American Diaries

MADDIE RETTA LAUREN

SANDERSVILLE, GEORGIA, C.S.A., 1864

—◆◆◆—

by Kathleen Duey

—◆◆◆—

Aladdin Paperbacks

New York London Toronto Sydney Singapore

For Richard
For Ever

First Aladdin Paperbacks edition, April 2000

Aladdin Paperbacks
An imprint of Simon & Schuster
Children's Publishing Division
1230 Avenue of the Americas
New York, NY 10020.

Designed by Steve Scott
The text for this book was set in Fairfield Light
Printed and bound in the United States of America
10 9 8 7 6 5 4 3 2 1
Library of Congress Catalog Card Number: 11901443
ISBN 0-689-83377-6

December 11, 1864

Almost sunrise, but I cannot go back to sleep. I finished sewing the ruffle I salvaged from my worn-out spring frock onto my yellow dress to hide the threadbare spots. It looks all right, more or less. Mama is so angry about the blockade. She says Northern women aren't patching and mending like we are. She says they have enough to eat, too.

We heard gunfire again last evening. I brought Ginger up to the barn this afternoon. Tomorrow as early as I can, I shall take her out to the old place in the swamp. The little corral is still standing outside Great-grandpa's old log house. No one could easily find the way in without knowing the place was there, and I think she will be safe. No filthy Yankee is going to take my gentle-hearted mare.

Mama would stop me if she knew, I am sure. She wouldn't want me riding out in the woods alone—and besides that, she has decided that there is no good purpose in trying to hide any of the horses. She may well be right . . . we have all heard the stories from Spencer's Branch and other places. People say the Yankees were enraged when they couldn't find horses, so they torched not only fields and barns, but the houses, too. Mama says better to lose the stock than to lose everything. And we have nowhere to hide so many horses, anyway, really. There are more than a hundred in the barns and paddocks. I will be lucky to get Ginger out to the little corral near Great-grandfather's house without being seen.

The smell of smoke is heavy in the air night and day. My throat is raw and sore from it. Everyone is on edge, bad-tempered, and worried about what each day shall bring. How can we not be? The Yankees are closer every day.

Yesterday afternoon we all rolled bandages again out of old cotton cloth. Mama will send Henry with the boxful to Captain Grim's wife, and she will see they get where they are needed. The whole time, looking out the parlor windows, we could see black smoke from the fires and I could hear the far-off gunfire, faint at this distance but still terrifying. Everyone is beginning to admit that we cannot win—even Mama, though she will not say it in so many words.

These arrogant Yankees, with their ports open and their ships' holds full of food and soap and candles coming in freely. Mama says they thought they would starve us out in a few months, but that they hadn't reckoned on the women.

It's true. Papa may be gone off to war, but Mama can run this place nearly as well as he can, maybe better in some ways. For nearly three years now, we have scraped and made do. Mama scorns even the smallest waste, and the servants have invented ways to stretch food from a little into enough.

I know Mama will have her heart broken the day the Yankees come, though. All of our slaves are fiercely loyal to her—but I have overheard even Jubal and Daisy whispering about Lincoln's soldiers, and I am sure that when the Yankees come, many will follow them. Who can blame them? Some say they will not be able to care for themselves, but I know they are wrong. Our Negroes will make out all right. Papa has made sure that most have learned trades beyond fieldwork. My dear Sarajane can read, and so can her sisters—though they hide it. I taught Sarajane when we were little. We used to pretend the well house was a schoolhouse and would sit for hours, using the dirt floor and a nail as paper and pen. Then she instructed Rose and Aster and maybe her parents as well, using my old books.

I can hear the roosters now and I can see the outlines of the oaks outside my window. We will be burying food and goods again today, I expect. Mama says the Yankees will not get what she has worn herself out saving up. She worked like a demon with her jam kettle and her salting crocks all summer. Not a single peach hit the ground, and when there was no sugar to use, she salted them instead and packed them in pickle crocks.

She feeds the hogs from table scraps and stable

spillings, and on the milk we couldn't make into cheese when the weather was too hot. And every day Granger and Randall take them into the woods to forage for themselves.

Mister Billy Yank might think he is better than we are, but he is wrong. We made our own soap yesterday, and a batch of ink so that Mama can keep on writing Papa, mailing the letters from Taber's store every Monday morning. And I kept out my little bit so that I may write here. I cramp my handwriting so small, but still I fill too many pages in this old order book. Paper is so scarce now—it scares me to think I will run out, that I won't have this private place to record my fears and hopes.

Mama says there is no point in crying over the Yankees beating us in the war, but I hear her crying every night. I know she misses Papa and fears for him as I do.

Mama says Lincoln will want to be king next, that being reelected president will not be enough for the man. Oh, how we hate him. The slaves revere him, though, I know. How strange that Sarajane, whom I have lived with and loved my whole life, can admire a man I hate. Of course, I hate Jefferson Davis, too, and Lee and all those South Carolina firebrands for leading us in this hopeless war. And now the Yankees are destroying everything. How long before we are refugees in the woods with no place to sleep?

Mr. Bryant was here yesterday, and I overheard him telling Mama that if the North had left us alone we would have gotten rid of slavery within a generation, anyway. Patience would have precluded the need for blood. He says Northern workers are the new slaves— wage slaves instead of chattel slaves. I wish Papa were here. I want to ask him what he thinks of all that. He was not for secession; he is fighting almost against his will, angry at the Yankees but almost as angry at the men who are so strongly secesh that they have torn the Union and caused us this bloody war.

Tim Bryant was with his father. He has gotten better with his crutches, but it is terrible and strange to see a young man with one leg. If only the twenty years we needed to end slavery on our own had come sooner— soon enough to save us all. No one with a heart can defend slavery, not even to the face they see in the looking glass every morning. Papa would scold me for this tirade, I know, but here, in my diary, I can say what I please. And if my grandchildren read it one day, I should like them to know even some of those who lived with slaves knew it was wrong.

Let them also know that this war is terrible. Every family I know has lost its men or had them come home without a limb or an eye or invalided some other way. The South may never recover from the loss of its young men, Mama says.

The Yankees have taken so much from us and will take more, but there is one thing I can perhaps prevent. Ginger, my own lovely mare—a sweeter, more willing horse never lived. She has been a gently handled lady's mount all her life. I will not allow some hooligan of a Yankee to whip and abuse her into harder work than she can stand. I won't permit her to be lashed into galloping against cannon fire, shot in battle. I don't care what it costs me. In the midst of all this misery, I find I can only help my horse? If this is my only possible victory against the Yankees, I mean to win it.

Mama is up now. I can hear her in the kitchen, talking to Daisy. They will be talking about Yankees, first thing, before either of them even looks out the door at the sunrise. Yankees have killed my cousins and friends and may yet kill my dear, Unionist father, who really doesn't disagree with them on much except their right to shove abolitionism down our throats. They have thrown a shadow over all my life, from here to my grave. Mama says the young men who live will be bitter and defeated all their lives.

This will be another long and dreary day, smelling the smoke from our neighbors' houses, waiting for the sound of the Yankee boots and gunfire.

CHAPTER ONE

Maddie opened her bedroom door silently and tiptoed into the hall. She crept past the stair landing, peeking down into the sitting room to make sure that her mother wasn't there. Once inside her parents' room, she moved the neat stack of quilting squares atop her mother's trunk and opened it slowly, careful not to let the domed top bang the wall.

Glancing at the door every few seconds, she rummaged downward in the folded stacks of clothing until she came to her brother's old things. Pulling out a pair of trousers that she was sure would fit her well enough, she felt a familiar tug of sadness. Johnny had died at barely thirteen years old, four years before, drowned in the pond swimming with the Thornton boys.

"And if he hadn't drowned," she whispered to herself, "he would have been a soldier by now, or at least in the junior reserve."

Her familiar sorrow thinking about Johnny's

death melted into a fresher pain—fear for her father. Every Confederate soldier was in even more danger than ever before. The tide of the war had turned forever. The senior reserve—men between ages forty-five and sixty—was beginning to serve in the regular ranks. No one had enough to eat, and in some places the refugees outnumbered the citizens. The Confederacy was fighting on, but everyone thought it futile now, a show of honor and stubborn pride more than any illusion that they might still somehow win.

Sliding the trousers on beneath her skirt hoops, Maddie wriggled the pants over her hips, then buttoned them over her corset and pulled at the waist. They were loose, but they would stay up. She rolled one of Johnny's white linen shirts in a tight wad and shoved it into the front of the trousers. Then, she pulled out his old cap. Seeing it very nearly made her cry. She tucked it in the trousers front with the shirt.

Her breath fluttery and uneven, Maddie closed the trunk and carefully replaced her mother's quilting squares. Going out, she peeked down the hall, opening the door an inch at a time until she was sure her mother was still downstairs. Then she ran back to her room, her bare feet light and cautious on the polished oak floor.

Once inside, she rolled up the trouser legs to put on stockings and laced on her lowest-heeled riding boots. Her hem would cover them well enough, and

Mama would have no reason to be staring at her feet.

Maddie fixed her long hair a little, tightening the bun and smoothing it as best she could. She reset her hairpins. Sarajane usually brushed her hair for her, but this morning Mama would have every one on the place hustling and bustling.

Breathless with the uneasiness in her heart, Maddie went back out into the hallway and walked more slowly than she wanted to, descending the stairs carefully, looking down at her skirts to see if the trousers and the bulk of the rolled-up shirt and cap were visible beneath her skirt. They weren't. She had on her smallest, everyday housedress hoops, but they were enough to hold the fabric of her dress away from her extra padding.

"Maddie Retta!" Mama scolded her as she entered the kitchen. "I was about to send Sarajane up to wake you on her next trip in from the springhouse."

Maddie shrugged, hoping her mother couldn't see the pink flush on her cheeks. Her heart was beating hard. She was not used to lying to her mother. Mama suddenly scrutinized her, her hands on her waist above the flare of her hoops. "Is that the best you can do today?"

Maddie looked down at her skirt. She had had a very specific reason for choosing the old cotton frock, but she couldn't tell her mother that. Blushing again, she said, "Yes, Mama, it is."

Mama sighed. "What if they came right now, Maddie? What if they just marched into the yard and—"

"Mama, I don't care what some old Yankees think of the way I'm dressed," Maddie interrupted. She frowned, staring at her mother's perfect silk housedress, then glanced up at her face. Mama's eyes were red-rimmed, and her cheeks were pale. "Did you sleep at all, Mama?"

"Very little." Mama pushed a stray lock of hair back from her face. "I kept thinking I heard them coming and I . . ." She trailed off and shook her head. "I am not sure which will turn out to be worse—the waiting, or what will happen when it is over."

Maddie nodded without speaking. Mama nudged her along, ushering her through the door. Daisy was busy at the sideboard. There were pans on the stove. "Sweet corn mush," she said without turning as Maddie came in. "And sausage."

Maddie felt her mouth water. She knew it would be delicious if Daisy made it. But it would also be scant fare. Mama had cut everyone's rations down to the bitter nub. Maddie was hungry all the time, it seemed. But sausage was a treat, no matter how little she was given. She would save half for Sarajane, wrap it in a napkin, and take it out to the springhouse. She fidgeted, hungrier than she liked to be. It seemed like it had been forever since they had truly had enough to eat.

The sausage crackled and spit in the pan. The smell of it browning was almost more than Maddie could bear. She swallowed and tried to put her mind onto other matters. She was going to have to get to the barns, then ride along the cotton fields all the way out to the woods without anyone seeing her. And it was not going to be easy.

"Smoke to the east and to the west today," Mama said in a voice that was as steady as if she were merely commenting on the weather.

Maddie nodded. "Can I help with something?"

Mama shook her head. "Daisy has it done. But I will work your legs off later, just you wait."

Daisy turned and shot a look at Maddie. Their eyes met in mutual distaste for another day of scurrying like ants in the rain.

"If we don't get everything covered and hidden, it will be gone," Mama said. Then she sighed. "It will likely be gone, anyway, but we have to try."

Daisy grimaced, talking over her shoulder as she stirred the steaming mush. "Demetrius said that they lined up the cows and shot them all on Dr. Haven's place."

Mama took in a quick breath. "Shot them? The milch cows?"

"Yes'm," Daisy said, shaking her head. "It was pitiful. What's wrong with those Yankees?"

Mama sat down heavily. "I wish your father were

here," she said so quietly that Maddie barely heard her above the popping of the grease in the sausage pan.

Maddie tried to think of something to say, something that would comfort her mother, but she couldn't.

"Maybe they will miss us altogether," Daisy said, breaking the silence.

Maddie smiled as Daisy turned, a bowl in her hands. "That could happen, Mama," she said as she took the bowl and smiled gratefully up at Daisy. "Maybe they will just march a little to the east and miss us."

"I would love to think so," Mama said, sitting down across from Maddie, pulling her coffee cup toward herself with the grace Maddie always envied. The cup had a pale, steaming liquid in it, Maddie saw, Daisy's bark tea. They hadn't been able to find real coffee for a long time.

"Oh, my Lord," Daisy murmured, and Maddie looked up to see her staring out the window.

"What is it?" Mama asked, her voice tight.

Daisy didn't answer for so long that Mama got up and went to the window to stand beside her. "Only five?" Mama said after a moment.

Daisy nodded, then shook her head. "Six."

"Six what?" Maddie demanded. "Six Yankees?"

Mama turned without speaking, and Maddie felt her stomach wrench. They were here already? The waiting was over and Ginger was still in the barn?

Maddie jumped up and tiptoed to peer over her mother's shoulder. A line of blue-coated soldiers were coming up the road.

"Six is enough," Mama said heavily. "It's like locusts, I imagine. First a few, then enough to destroy everything. Quick," she said to Daisy. "Get the food put away."

Maddie felt her heart sink even though she knew it was foolish to pine about breakfast when the Yankees were coming.

"Here," Daisy said as she whirled around the kitchen, wrapping the mush pot and sliding it into the oven. "Here, child."

Maddie turned to look. Daisy was handing her two of the sausages. They were almost too hot to hold, but Maddie ate them quickly, wiping her hands on the dishrag. Then she spun around to scoop up the silver to put back into the cypress silver chest.

"Here," Mama said suddenly, motioning.

Maddie helped her lift the silver chest down from the sideboard, and they slid it beneath the baking table, pushing it all the way back against the wall.

Standing up, Maddie wished for just one more sausage, then guiltily remembered that she hadn't saved so much as a morsel for Sarajane.

"See to the coffeepot," Mama instructed her. Sara put it down next to the silver chest, then stepped back. Both were in the shadows, impossible to see unless someone got down on their hands and knees. She blinked and looked around, seeing the kitchen as though it were unfamiliar—the way a Yankee might see it. It was immaculate. Daisy and Mama kept it so clean, anyway, that it hadn't taken more than clearing things away to make it shine. It looked as though no one had prepared food in it for days.

"The smell," Mama said.

Daisy nodded and flung open the windows, sliding the sashes up as high as they could go. Maddie walked over to stare out the window at the Yankees as they trotted their horses at an easy pace, coming closer, their faces lit by the first sun of the day.

CHAPTER TWO

"Maddie!" Mama hissed.

Glancing at her mother, then back at the Yankees, Maddie could hear only the beating of her own heart for several seconds. Here they were. After months of fearing their arrival, here they were, riding along like anyone else, and approaching the house calmly as if they were invited guests. The eeriness of the whole scene stunned her into motionless silence.

"Maddie!"

The ferocity of her mother's voice freed Maddie from her paralysis, and she turned. "Yes, Mama?"

"Run upstairs and get your clothing out of your armoire. At least put all but one or two dresses beneath your bed. Leave out your oldest ones." Mama pushed her hair back from her face. "I thought we would have another day or two." She made a shooing motion with her hands. "Go!"

"Yes, Mama," Maddie said, nodding, but she still

couldn't move. She stood stalk-still and watched as her mother faced Daisy.

"Send one of the boys out to the quarter. Tell him to get everyone up and remind them of what we have talked about and practiced. No matter what anyone is asked, no one is to tell the Yankees where our food is hidden. No one. It will not affect their freedom when and if it comes. But we will all starve this winter if the Yankees take our stores now."

"Yes'm," Daisy said, and Maddie could see both fear and excitement in her eyes. No one knew what to expect from the Yankees, not even the slaves they meant to free.

"Maddie!" Mama exploded. "Don't stand there another second!" Maddie mumbled an apology as she followed Daisy out the kitchen door, then veered off across the sitting room to go up the stairs two at a time, feeling the unfamiliar bulges of her brother's old clothes with every step.

How lucky she was that she was already dressed for what she needed to do. If she had waited, she would have had no chance at all to save Ginger. She had little enough now. With the Yankees here, it was going to be even harder to slip out. Would there be more soon, riding up through the woods behind the house? Maddie shivered even though it wasn't cold this morning. The Yankees would stop her if they saw her. She had to think of some way to leave without alerting them or worrying her mother.

From her bedroom window Maddie couldn't see the road that ran along the front of Grand Oaks—she could only see straight out the back of the house. She stood, drawing in quick breaths, staring past the lines of low-roofed log cabins that formed the slaves' quarter. The unplowed cotton fields behind them were empty. Maddie scanned the edge of the woods nearly a half mile away. She couldn't see any riders, but knew that meant nothing.

A flicker of movement caught her eye; it was shirttails flying. Even from this distance she recognized Albert's tall, lanky form as he burst from the far end of the pecan orchard and angled toward the quarter. He was running like the wind, with both fear and joy lifting his feet, she was sure. She envied him fiercely for an instant. At least there was a great good that would come for him out of this terrible war. For the slaves, something brave and fine was beginning. For her and her family, there would be only the taste of ashes.

Forcing herself to turn around, Maddie went to her armoire and flung open the doors. She lifted out her dresses one by one and stacked them on the carpet. Once the armoire was empty except for her three oldest and most worn day dresses, she folded the whole stack in half and dragged it over to her bed. It was hard to shove the yards of bombazine, moiré silk, and lace beneath her bed frame, but she managed, then stood up, scanning her room for other valuables. As she stood motionless, a sudden pounding on the front door rang out, loud even upstairs. The racket could not be from a man's fist knocking on the polished oak of the door, she realized. It sounded as though someone was pounding on it with a gunstock.

Maddie's heart leaped, then skipped a beat, and she turned slowly, staring at the open door of her room. The pounding came a second time. Maddie heard her mother cough, then the familiar creaking of the door hinges. Maddie crept out into the hallway, then to the top of the stairs, listening hard.

"Good morning, ma'am," came the Yankee's voice. "As you might already know, we have been authorized to take any rations we need in order to support the Union army." He said it evenly and reasonably, as though it were out of the question that Mama would oppose his right to anything she owned.

"Ma'am?" a second voice added. "Did you hear Corporal Martin?"

"She's trying to act like she doesn't have food," a third voice chimed in. The words were followed by a rough, uncivilized laugh. "We have been authorized, ma'am."

Maddie found herself standing with her back pressed against the wall, her mouth dry and her heart thumping against her ribs. These sounded like the worst kind of Yankees, lowborn and bound to prove that they had learned nothing since that unlucky day.

"You folks must have a silver tea service, am I right?" one of the voices inquired.

Maddie could hear her mother make a sharp, angry sound. "What is your business here in my home?" Mama inquired coldly.

Maddie crept down the first few stairs, straining to hear the answer. For a long moment, there was none. The Yankees laughed. It was a grating sound, like a donkey's braying.

"Billy, she wants to know what our business is," one of them said loudly.

Maddie went down the last five stairs, her knees weak and trembly. It seemed wrong that Mama had to face these rude men all by herself. Papa would have sent them running, she was sure of that. She ached to have her father home, where he belonged, protecting them.

"Just don't argue with us, ma'am," the first Yankee said deliberately.

Maddie forced herself to walk forward, her eyes on the kitchen door, angling her path so that she could see through it. She stared at her mother's back, then blinked and lifted her eyes to take in the Yankees. Three of them stood in close order on the porch, half inside the doorway. The others were at the bottom of the porch steps, holding their horses' reins. They looked weirdly calm, implacable, as though this were a simple thing they did every day of the world—banging on strangers' doors and threatening to take all they owned.

Of the Yankees Maddie could see best, two were average-looking men, except for the fact that they were dirty and ill-kempt. But the third had dark, wild eyes and a look of deep anger on his face. He was the one who spoke up next. "Ma'am, we are tired and hungry and we will be on our way quick enough if you cooperate. If you don't . . ." He put his hand meaningfully on the grip of a pistol he carried in his belt.

Maddie caught her breath, but Mama was standing tall and straight, looking up at the men. "I think you had better leave us alone here," she said evenly. The three Yankees burst into laughter at her bravado, and Maddie wanted to make them stop more than anything she had ever wanted in her life. How dare they mock her mother? How dare they mock anyone at all? This was not their land; it was not their country. Nor would it ever be, no matter what they thought.

Maddie fought an impulse to pull her mother away from the rude, ugly-mannered men, to drag her upstairs, where she would be safer. But beneath her impulse she realized what her mother was doing. Every minute she spent arguing with the men, the just-awakened folks in the quarter would have another little bit of time to gather their wits and react to the presence of the Yankees with calm and caution.

"I suppose you have a ham or two put away somewhere?" one of the Yankees said. His voice was sly and sweet, as though he were a beggar wheedling passersby on a street corner.

"We have very little food," Mama said sternly. "And we will need every bit of it to get everyone through the winter. There are children here, sir, and elderly who depend on me," she added, and her voice was strained.

The Yankee seemed not to have heard. He stepped around Mama and stood looking into the house. He nodded absently at Maddie, and his eyes meeting hers made her heart constrict. "Come on in," he said loudly, gesturing at her. "We were just talking to your mother for a minute or two."

Maddie heard the false warmth in the man's voice. Was this all a game to him, no more serious than playing a round of King's Base or Miley Bright? Did he think it was fun to frighten women and girls?

"Come on in," the man repeated, and this time his voice held no false warmth at all.

"She's just a girl," one of the others chided.

He rounded on his friend. "And you don't know how many brothers she has, or if there are Rebs out in the corn shed and she is just the one to go wake them up and tell them we're here." He looked Maddie up and down. "She's old enough to shoot a rifle."

"Nonsense," Mama said instantly. "What would I be if I put my own daughter at risk?"

The wild-eyed Yankee looked her up and down. "A cowardly secesh Rebel?" he asked, and the three men lapsed into laughter again. The wild-eyed one straightened, wiping his sleeve across his mouth, his eyes watery with mirth.

For the first time, Maddie realized that they had been drinking. They must have stolen someone's brandy, or taken bottles of wine from someone's cellar.

"Get in here," the wild-eyed one said again. Maddie stepped into the kitchen doorway and stopped. Mama did not turn to look at her.

One of the Yankee's companions tugged at his sleeve. "Aw, Billy—"

"Get your hands off me," Billy said irritably. "Let's just get the food and go. They aren't that far behind us now."

"Your officers?" Mama said sharply. "Is that who you mean? Aren't you with your companies?"

Billy hawked and spit on the floor, and Maddie cringed. It was the most offensive thing she had ever seen a man do. He stared straight at Mama, and his eyes were cold and hard. "Ma'am, it is none of your business where or who our officers are."

Mama raised her head and stared back at him, and even though Maddie couldn't see her mother's face from where she stood, she could easily imagine the proud, stubborn look the Yankee was getting. He spat on the floor a second time. Mama did not move a fraction of an inch; it was as though his manners were so bad that she refused to remark upon them or even *notice* them—as though she would no more deign to correct him any more than she would correct a pig for wallowing in mud.

"Lady, give us enough to feed the six of us for the rest of the day and we won't set your house afire."

Maddie caught her breath once more, but again, Mama did not lower her head or speak. The Yankee raised his hand as if to strike her, then lowered it again.

"If I am ordered by proper Union officers to give over my supplies, I shall consider doing so," Mama said slowly, enunciating every word as though she were shaping it for all the ages to follow. "But I will not turn anything over to freebooters and renegades who are looting for their own profit and adventure." Mama pulled in a breath and straightened her shoulders. "I have to think about feeding one hundred and five people, sir, including the old and the babies. I am responsible for all of us making it through this long winter."

The third man, who had been silent the whole time, suddenly stepped forward. "Billy, come on." He cleared his throat and looked behind himself. "Maybe she's just stalling so her menfolk can get here and shoot us as we come out."

Billy laughed, a short, pained sound.

"Ma'am," said the third man in a low, pleasing voice. "Just give us some food and we'll leave and be out of your way."

"I see no reason to give my husband's enemies my hospitality," Mama said stubbornly.

Swearing, Billy lifted his hand again as though he was about to hit Mama. Once more, she didn't move.

"Let's just go see what we can find," the quiet man said.

Billy's sharp face eased into a grin. "Sure. Why waste time trying to get this mean old woman to give us what any decent human being would give without even being asked. You can smell the breakfast they had. Anyone else would be hospitable."

"My boys are all about the place," Mama told him evenly. "Off at their chores, but they'll be back."

Maddie noticed a tiny motion of the hemline of Mama's skirt. It was trembling, a barely noticeable vibration. Mama's knees were shaking beneath her full, hooped skirt, but her chin was as high as it had been from the beginning. "They are all armed and they know the land here like you never will," Mama added. She tilted her head. "We won't be able to fight off the whole of Sherman's horde when it comes," she said regretfully. "But we can handle six stray Yankees any morning. Can't we, Maddie?"

The question startled Maddie, and she pulled in a quick breath. "Try us and see," she said, amazed that the words came out of her mouth in understandable form. She was not as brave as her mother was and she never would be. Mama half turned and gave her an approving glance, then extended her arm like a gracious hostess, escorting guests out.

"If you gentlemen wouldn't mind, we have much work to do here today. We are going to plow our cotton fields and pray that the war will be over in time for us to plant."

Maddie watched the men exchange glances, hesitating.

"Wait long enough and my sons will be back from their errands. They'll have sense enough to keep hidden, then follow you down the road a ways. Union men who steal have a way of getting lost in these woods."

Maddie exhaled when Billy jammed his hat back on his head and turned to go out. His companions were right behind him. Maddie heard Billy curse when the three who had stayed outside began to ask questions. They all seemed to defer to Billy, though, and when he reined his horse around toward the road, they went with him.

"That was closer than I like so early in the day,"

Mama said, and now Maddie could hear a quaver in her voice.

"You were wonderful, Mama."

Maddie saw her mother shake her head. "Just stubborn. I thought for a moment there that they would as soon hurt us as not. But deep down, most men have some decency left." She smoothed her hair. "Maddie, run out to the barns and tell Jake and Zeke to take the milch cows out to the eastside pasture and leave them there. I intend to leave the horses and mules where they are. I don't want the house burned down. And we can afford to lose horses better than cows now." She patted Maddie's cheek, and Maddie knew she was apologizing in advance if anything happened to Ginger.

"Mama?" Maddie began, intending to tell her mother what she had planned. Then she hesitated, wondering if she should take two or three horses. She might be able to hide two or three animals, but not all of them. She bit at her lip. The marsh's wet soil would show the tracks too clearly—anyone might notice a wide trail this time of year.

"I'll be helping Daisy get the flour and sugar buried in the side yard," Mama said, interrupting her thoughts. "And I'll be sending the house boys on errands as I think of things we ought to be doing. We probably have precious little time left."

Maddie nodded. At least Mama was sending her

in the direction she needed to go. She wouldn't need to fib. "I'll be careful," she promised, meaning it fervently. She was scared. But she couldn't let that stop her.

Mama nodded briskly. "I will depend upon it. And if you see anyone you don't know and trust, come straight back to the house and get Zeke or Jake to go with you for protection if you can."

Maddie nodded. "I will, Mama." She watched her mother turn on her heel and stride out of the kitchen, calling for Daisy. Maddie sighed, hoping that she could be as brave as her mother was. One thing was for sure: Mama wouldn't allow Maddie to ride Ginger into the woods alone if she knew beforehand. But afterward, if everything came out all right, Mama would likely forgive her; she would understand.

CHAPTER THREE

Maddie ran through the sitting room and passed into the long hall that divided the back half of the house. This part was the old house, the one her grandfather had built when Papa was still a little boy. Papa had had the front part added on just before Johnny was born.

At the thought of her brother, Maddie felt the usual twinge of pain in her heart. Johnny had been so good-hearted, such a laughing, happy, high-humored boy. Other girls complained about their brothers being bothersome, but Maddie had only loved her own. And she missed him every day.

Pushing the back door open, Maddie went out slowly, scanning the horizon as far as she could see. There were low hills on the north end of the plantation, but in this direction, the land was flat as a tabletop. She couldn't see past the barns from the porch except to see that the sky was still dark with smoke. It smelled stronger outside than it had inside.

Maddie thought for a second about going back in, running up the stairs to her bedroom window so she could see farther, but then she decided not to give her mother time to ask someone else to carry her orders to Zeke and Jake. She didn't have time to think up another excuse to get outside. She had to get Ginger out to the old corral, then get back to the house before Mama had time to worry—and before any more Yankees came. She glanced at the sky. The sun was well up now, and it looked odd, rouged by the haze of smoke. She could manage the ride to the old place in about an hour, and then it would take her about twice that to walk home again. Three hours. Mama was going to be so busy. Maddie might not even be missed.

Hitching up her skirt, Maddie ran across the lawn, going around the rose bed that bordered the yard along the back. The springhouse door was ajar, and she stopped long enough to push it closed, lowering the latch bar in one quick motion. She was about to run again when she heard a familiar shout from inside.

"Sarajane?" she said through the door, then lifted the latch to reopen it. "I'm so sorry! I thought you were finished and you'd left the door open by mistake."

Sarajane came out smiling, but it was a nervous smile. "I was supposed to get everything moved three days ago and I didn't half finish yesterday. Everyone has me running errands, and I barely got to work. Your mama is going to be red-faced if she catches me."

Maddie reached out to touch Sarajane's cheek. From when they were little it had been like this. Maddie put things off and then had to work too fast to get her chores done. Sarajane did everything completely the opposite. She would do things so carefully and well that if anyone tried to make her work fast, she got flustered. Miss Rush and Miss Tarry, Mama had called them when they were younger.

"Just hurry, Miss Tarry," Maddie said aloud, and Sarajane smiled. Then the smile faded, and Maddie could tell she was wondering whether or not to say something. After a few seconds, she drew in a deep breath.

"Those Yankees," she began. "Albert said Daisy said they looked mean. Did they look mean?"

Maddie nodded. "Mean and low and rough-mannered. I think some are much better than these, but maybe not. Mama called them 'renegades.'" She stared at Sarajane, longing to ask her if she would follow the Yankees if her parents did. There were so many stories about the huge, crowded camps of Negro people following the Yankee armies around. Maddie realized she was staring.

"What?" Sarajane asked, her eyes widening in the way that made them crinkle at the corners.

Maddie tried to think of some way to ask. Sarajane was her oldest and closest friend. They had grown up in the same crib, practically, because Sarajane's mother had nursed Maddie, too, when Mama got sick with fever and lost her milk.

"Will you stay here?" Maddie managed, shifting her weight from one foot to the other.

"My daddy says we will for a time, anyway," Sarajane said matter-of-factly, as though there was nothing special or discomfiting about the question at all. "He says he's afraid to just take off to somewhere he's never been before so close after everything's been all torn up by the war."

"I am glad," Maddie said quietly. "I can't think what it would be like to never see you again."

Sarajane smiled again, her wonderful, slightly crooked smile. "Your mama said we could work for her after freedom if we wanted. Papa says that might be all right with him."

Maddie hugged her and kissed her cheek. "I meant to save you some of the sausage, but the Yankees came and I was so scared and preoccupied, I just ate it up and—"

"Don't you worry about it," Sarajane said politely, but Maddie could see the shadow of longing in her eyes.

"I really am sorry," Maddie added, hoping that making the apology longer would make it better.

The sound of distant gunfire made them both stiffen. "We should hurry," Sarajane said. Maddie could see tears in the corners of her eyes. Everybody was weepy for different reasons these days, and Sarajane had always hated crying in front of anyone.

Maddie nodded. "Maybe they won't come here." She saw Sarajane's face and bit her lip. "To burn us out, I mean. Maybe they won't ruin the plantation."

Sarajane nodded slowly. "Pray for that."

Maddie looked straight into Sarajane's eyes. "I will. Be careful."

"Of the Yankees?"

"Yes," Maddie said, turning to go. "The ones this morning were not gentlemen at all. They threatened Mama. I think they were renegades or deserters, or something just as bad."

Sarajane nodded and Maddie started away, her mind a tumble of thoughts. Then she turned back. "Do me a favor?"

"Yes, Missy Maddie," Sarajane answered.

"Tell Mama I have some extra things to do out at the barn, will you?" Maddie asked. "Tell her I will be a while."

Sarajane nodded and Maddie thanked her, then started off again. She felt strange, like a piece of dandelion fluff in the wind. She had no idea what to say to any of the Negro people she had known all her life. She wanted to tell them that she understood them wanting to be free. But how could she know what it felt like not to be? She loved some of them as much as her own family. Sarajane was the closest friend she would ever have, almost her sister. But there seemed to be an ocean between them now. Maybe there always had been? The thought hurt.

Maddie passed the chicken coop, then across the footbridge that Papa had built over the creek. Holding up her skirts again, she angled to the right, ducking under the low limbs of the pecan trees until she came out the far side of the orchard. Then she climbed over the fence to go through the cow pasture because it was shorter than going around the quill-work of garden patches that ran along the front of the cabins.

She kept her head up as much as she could without stepping in cow manure, looking around with nearly every step. The last thing she wanted was to be surprised out in the open by a bunch of Yankees.

She veered again, waving at Auntie Mary and Albert when she saw them. "Where's Zeke and Jake?" she shouted, slowing.

Auntie Mary waved one long, thin arm. "Up in the barns somewhere, I suspect."

Nodding and smiling to show that nothing was wrong, Maddie walked along the edge of the gardens past the cabins, then turned right up the path that led past the cow barns, breaking back into a run until she came to the pigpens. As Maddie slowed to catch her breath, the huge sows were snuffling at their troughs, nosing the last bits of their sweet potatoes and milk.

The biggest York sow and one or two of the others had gotten out a few times over the last month. The pens needed repair, and Mama hadn't gotten around to assigning anyone the job. There was so much to do to get ready for the Yankees coming that every hand had been needed to preserve and hide food. Loose gate latches were less important now.

Still breathing hard, Maddie broke back into a run. There wouldn't be anyone in the cow barns this late. Milking was long over, done by lantern light. The big tin cans would be standing deep in cold creek water in the cooling house built on the creek where it passed above the cow paddocks.

Following along the edge of the creek-side cotton field, Molly came to the first of the horse barns. She could hear the horses moving restlessly in their stalls, whinnying. She slowed to a walk and tried to calm her breathing so she could hear better. Something had the horses excited. Maybe the six Yankees had doubled back. Or maybe there were others coming in from the woods.

Maddie looked around, scanning the edge of the cotton field back to the quarter, then looking at the woods before the field to the north. Most likely the horses had just caught the scent of a raccoon in the pines behind the barns. She shivered. There was no way to know for sure.

Maddie walked forward cautiously, keeping to the shadows of the oak trees that lined the path. She couldn't see any sign of Yankees, and she let out a long breath but kept her eyes moving constantly, scanning the barns and the paddocks across from them.

Then she heard Zeke's voice; he was shouting something at Jake. The familiar sound of the two men arguing eased Maddie's heart and made her smile. Everything else might be upside down this morning, but Zeke and Jake were disagreeing over something as usual. They were brothers, born a year apart, and they had argued from the cradle on, Mama always said. Maddie listened. It was about a bay brood mare that had been off her feed. Jake wanted to try a bran mash. Zeke didn't want to waste the bran on a mare that wasn't colicked, just off her feed. They didn't have much left, and who knew what they might need it for?

It was a pure comfort to Maddie that they were shouting at each other—it seemed so every day, it somehow made it seem possible that the Yankees would not come, that they would ride a different route and miss the homeplace altogether. Maybe the six renegades had been trying to stay out of General Sherman's way and were skirting Sherman's army's main path.

Buoyed by these thoughts, Maddie hesitated, wanting more than anything to explain what she was going to do to Jake and Zeke. If they told any messenger Mama might send that Maddie was working with them in the barns, as she often did, things would be easier. But she knew she couldn't ask them to lie. If things did go badly, she didn't want either of them to feel as if they should have stopped her. This decision was hers alone. And whatever happened, the blame would be hers alone as well.

Maddie spotted Jake at the well, pumping buckets full of water, facing away from her. She couldn't see Zeke, but his voice was coming from the farthest barn, where the brood mares were kept until they foaled. They shouted back and forth twice more, then Maddie heard Zeke start singing. Hymns were often his way of ending debates with his brother. It bothered Jake mightily, but there was nothing he could do about it. This morning, Zeke's selection was one of Maddie's favorite Negro songs. She heard it chiming forth from the praise house at the end of the cabin row where services were held every Sunday morning.

"Mary and Marthy, feed my lambs," Zeke's voice rang out, drowning out Jake's angry protest with his beautiful baritone choir voice.

"Mary and Marthy, feed my lambs . . ."

Jake shouted once more, but Zeke's strong voice muffled whatever he was trying to say. Maddie picked up her skirts and came forward, walking up the middle of the road. After a moment, Jake turned and saw her. "Morning, Miss Maddie," he said, smiling at her without parting his lips. Jake was missing two teeth from a horse kick, and he hated to show the gaps the accident had left.

"Good morning," Maddie called back. "Albert tell you about the Yankees?"

Jake looked startled, then confused.

"Did you get up here before dawn?"

He nodded. "When it was still black as pitch out. We have three mares close to foaling."

Maddie sighed. So they were acting normally because they had no idea they shouldn't be. "Yankees came to the door just at sunrise," she said as evenly as she could. She could see Jake fighting to keep his face sorrowful and worried. "They'll be back, never fear," she assured him, and his expression changed to excitement, which he then tried to hide. The result was a ghastly expression of stiff and painful resolve. "It was only six to start with."

"Your mama run them off?"

"Yes. They were freebooters, Jake, and half drunk." Maddie felt torn between laughter and tears, staring at him as his eyes twinkled but he held his mouth firm and straight. He didn't care if the Yankees were eight feet tall and had green ears, so long as they came and brought freedom with them. She cleared her throat. "Mama wants you to take the milch cows and turn them out in the eastside pasture."

Jake nodded, looking relieved to have anything to talk about besides Yankees. Maddie wondered if he would follow Sherman's destroying army as the soldiers marched through. Maybe, she decided. *Probably.* Jake was not much above twenty and he wasn't a family man yet. He had nothing to tie him here. She wondered if she would ever see him again. Zeke was a little older and had a wife and a little son over on Tileys' place. He would probably not follow the soldiers. But would he leave once the war was over? Maybe they all would, Sarajane's family included.

"Up in the eastside pasture," Jake said softly, echoing her words. "Are you certain?"

Brought back from her thoughts, Maddie nodded. "Yes."

"It's still swampy and full of snakes up there with the warm weather we've had this past month."

Maddie nodded again, understanding her mother's order for the first time. The country itself might keep the Yankees out. "Mama probably figures one or two lost to snakebite is better than all of them lost to the Yankees. They are shooting cattle, Jake."

Jake's eyes went wide, and she could see that the idea of it upset him as much as it did her. "That ain't right," he said softly.

"Not right or necessary, Mama says."

"They will starve half of us in our first winter of freedom," Jake said, then glanced sidelong at her.

Maddie nodded to show that she didn't mind him saying what they all knew was becoming truer by the day. The only question was how much longer the South could hold out with its farms burned and its people weak from too little food.

"I'll take them up alone," Jake said. "Will you tell Zeke where I've gone?"

Maddie nodded, wishing she could think of some way for them both to go. "I'll keep an eye on things here if you want his help."

Jake shook his head. "No. Your mama will want you back up at the house. You go visit Ginger yet?"

She shook her head.

"She was looking for you this morning. She always noses my pockets looking for carrots, and I tell her that's you that brings the carrots, not me. But that mare, she clings to her faith in all pockets, anyway—like an old Baptist woman with water. Most times, it works out for her, you see."

Maddie laughed with him. She could see everything in his eyes that she had seen in Sarajane's: fear; joy; fierce longing.

"I don't hate you," he said suddenly. "Or your parents."

Maddie stared at him, realizing that he was uneasy saying it, was taking the risk because he was fond of her. "Thank you, Jake," she said, unable to think of any other response.

He didn't answer, but looked out toward the woods. "Remember to tell Zeke I'll be back?"

Maddie nodded. "I will."

He picked up the water bucket and disappeared inside the first barn. Maddie heard horses inside whickering eager greetings. Every horse in the stables loved Zeke and Jake. Even the mules thought kindly of the two gentle-voiced men. They were always patient, always kind. True horsemen, Papa always said, were born, not made.

Before Jake could come back out of the double doors into the sunshine, Maddie hurried toward the foaling barn, then slowed again, glancing back to smile and wave. She only wanted Jake to think she was going to go talk to Zeke. That wasn't where she was going at all.

CHAPTER FOUR

As soon as Jake was preoccupied gathering the cattle into the top paddock, Maddie came back down the road, glancing behind herself to make sure Zeke hadn't come out of the foaling barn that stood at the end of the row. Ducking quickly into the third barn's big double doors, Maddie was blinded for a moment by the dim interior.

"Ginger?"

There was a startled, quiet whicker. Maddie's eyes were adjusting to the light, and she saw the tall buckskin mare put her head over the stall. "Hey, Miss Pretty," Maddie said quietly. Ginger whickered again.

Working as quickly as she could, Maddie ran to get her tack from behind the hayrick, where she had hidden it the night before. She came back carrying Ginger's bridle and her sidesaddle, glad Mama had insisted that Jake not do this for her every time, that she needed to be able to saddle her own horse if need be.

Ginger was skittish, and Maddie knew the mare

could feel her own nervousness. Maddie tried to move slowly and smoothly, as Jake had taught her from the time she was a little girl, but it was hard. Her hands were trembling. She tried to steady her uneasy breathing so Ginger wouldn't get the message that everything in the world was wrong.

"It's like a telegraph," Jake had always said. "You send a message to the horse every second. The way you stand, the way you breathe."

With the echo of Jake's teaching in her mind, Maddie tried hard to make the message she was sending to Ginger a calm one as she slipped the bridle on. Ginger took the snaffle bit easily and lowered her head to make slipping the crownpiece over her ears easier. "I'm going to go hide you in a safe place," Maddie murmured. "We'll gallop out to the old corral, then I'll walk home."

Ginger turned and blew warm, hay-scented breath across Maddie's cheek, then pawed at the ground with a front hoof. Maddie patted her, thinking furiously. Maybe she should take a second horse to ride home on. It would sure be faster.

Maddie considered it. Two horses missing would look like the work of those stray Yankees or some other thief. Finally, she shook her head. Two horses gone would only arouse suspicion faster. Anyone seeing only Ginger's stall empty would just assume Maddie had gone on some errand for Mama.

Maddie turned to get her saddle, then stopped, midmotion. If she was going to masquerade as a boy, she could hardly ride a sidesaddle. And all the other saddles were in the tack room—in the foaling barn! She felt sudden tears stinging at the back of her eyes. If she had been silly enough not to think of this, what else had she forgotten to plan for? She would have to ride bareback. She knew she could; she had done it many times when she was little, but it would feel odd.

Ginger shook her head, jingling the brass rings on the bridle. Maddie caught at the reins to still the noise, then stood motionless, listening. Zeke wasn't singing now. And if he had heard any commotion and came to check, he would never allow her to ride off by herself.

Maddie set her sidesaddle over the top stall rail and wrapped Ginger's reins loosely around the one below it. Then she set about changing herself into a boy. First she ran to peek out the double doors at the sunlit road. She still couldn't hear Zeke—but she couldn't see him, either. And Jake would not be back for a long time. The eastside pasture was a good, long walk, and the cows would want to amble along, grazing at the fencerow weeds.

Relieved that Zeke wasn't out of the foaling barn yet, Maddie turned back into the barn. She dithered a moment, then decided to change inside Ginger's stall. It felt entirely too immodest to simply pull her dress off in the center aisle. The stall was at least a little darker.

"If anyone comes, you let me know," she whispered to Ginger as she stepped into the deep straw bedding, her brother's clothes over her arm. Fingers awkward with her frantic hurry, she unbuttoned her dress and slid it off over her head, then untied her hoops and let them fall. She struggled out of her corset and shivered in the cool morning air as she finally lifted it off.

The shirt was warm from being next to her belly, and she buttoned it gratefully, the linen feeling foreign through just the thin cloth of her chemise. Careful to leave her pinned-up bun intact, she pulled the cap down tight over her ears. Last, she rolled up her clothes and gathered her hoops and opened the stall gate.

The instant Maddie emerged from the stall, Ginger snorted and threw her head back.

"It's me, Ginger," Maddie assured the startled mare quietly. "It's just me." Skeptical, Ginger lowered her head and pulled in a deep breath, making sure Maddie's scent was right. When it was, she shook her head, jingling the bridle again. Maddie grabbed the reins, patting Ginger's smooth neck, every nerve in her body tense and waiting for the sound of Zeke's footsteps. She stood still for a long moment, waiting, but no sound came.

Patting Ginger's neck a moment longer to make

sure that the mare would stand steady and quiet, Maddie finally ran to hide her dress in the hayrick, collapsing her hoops into a bundle of slim steel rings that slid beneath the wooden bin, where no one would ever find them.

She unwrapped Ginger's reins and led the mare toward the double doors. What would she do if Jake came now? Explain? That was no longer possible. Nor could she just ignore him and ride away. Her mother would never forgive him for it. Somehow she had to slip away unnoticed.

Ginger came quietly enough, but her head was high, eager to be out of the barn, to gallop on the roads for sheer pleasure the way they always had.

"This morning is different," Maddie warned her in a whisper. "This morning we have to be quiet at first, then we have to think about what kind of trail we are leaving behind."

Ginger whuffled her nostrils as though she had understood. Maddie pulled her to a stop just inside the double doors. Slowly, stepping forward a few inches at a time, Maddie peered out again. The path was empty.

She took a step into the sunshine, Ginger coming with her. Then the sound of Zeke's ringing baritone made her freeze. He was coming out of the foaling barn, singing to himself. Maddie pivoted and backed Ginger into the shadows of the barn.

"Jake?" Zeke shouted suddenly.

Maddie pulled Ginger around and led her up the aisle to her stall. The confused mare shook her head, resisting Maddie enough to register her protest at being put back in her stall. Maddie whispered apologies, but her pull on the reins was relentless. Slowly, as though her hooves were weighted, Ginger stepped inside. Maddie dropped the reins and shoved at the stall gate, closing it just as Zeke's shadow crossed the doorway.

"You in there?" he shouted. "Jake?"

Maddie held her breath. If he came in, she would have to hide somehow. If he saw her dressed like this—

"Jake!" Zeke shouted. He sounded irritated. "Are you upset with me? Over what I said about the bran mash?"

Maddie tried to breathe silently. Ginger stood as still as stone, her head up and her ears forward as though she were trying to unravel the mystery of the silly humans who were part of her life. Maddie could imagine her thinking. Humans usually answered shouts. So what was wrong with these two this morning, one shouting, the other not answering even when the shouting was loud and close?

"Hush now," Maddie breathed close to the mare's neck. "Just be still, Ginger."

"Jake? Answer me!" There was a sound of irritation following the clipped demand.

Maddie heard footsteps. He was coming in! She turned Ginger slightly, so that the mare's rump was toward the stall gate. If Zeke noticed the bridle, he would discover Maddie soon after.

"What in the world?" Zeke said quietly, so close that Maddie stiffened. She heard a scraping sound, and her heart hammered inside her chest. He was ten feet away from her, standing just beyond the stall rails. He was pulling her saddle down from the top rail. She could only hope that his eyes were still sun dazzled, that he couldn't see clearly in the dim barn yet.

"That silly Mistress Maddie of yours left the saddle where you could chew it," he said, addressing Ginger. She held her head higher at the sound of his voice, and Maddie had to hold the bridle tightly to keep her from turning to face Zeke. She shifted, stamping one hoof.

"Easy, girl," Zeke said. "I'll get you some grain in two minutes. Just let me put this saddle where it belongs and see if I can find that fool brother of mine. . . ."

His voice trailed off, and Maddie knew he had turned and was walking back up the aisle between the stalls. She waited until he was out of the barn and then exhaled. This wasn't going to work. She couldn't just lead Ginger out into the bright sun on the chance that Zeke wouldn't come back out at just the wrong second and see her riding off. He might even hear Ginger's hoofbeats and come looking to see who was there.

Wishing desperately that Zeke had gone with Jake to move the cows, Maddie tried to think. In the distance, she heard a pig squeal and almost smiled as an idea came to her. The sows. They always went toward the gardens around the quarter when they got out. When they did, Auntie Mary or Granger usually sent a child to fetch Zeke and Jake for help. The sows knew exactly where the garden patches were. They would raise exactly the kind of commotion she needed to ride away without anyone noticing. And since the gardens were mostly winter-barren now, anyway, no harm would be done.

Tying Ginger's reins around the rails at the back of the stall, Maddie faced her. She patted the mare's forehead, and then rubbed her jaw gently. "You stay here, Ginger," she whispered. "I will come back as quick as I can."

Holding her breath, Maddie opened the stall gate and went out, hurrying toward the wide double doors. The sun was shining inside now, thick, dust-heavy columns of light. She slowed just enough to look toward the tack barn, then, when she was sure that Zeke had not come out, she sprinted to the deep shade on the far side of the road. Staying as close to the tree trunks as she could, she raced toward the pigpens. For a few seconds she was aware of an unearthly feeling of lightness, then realized that the strange sensation came from the absence of her hoops and skirts.

CHAPTER FIVE

The biggest sow, a foul-tempered York, looked up as Maddie pounded up to the low plank fence. The instant the gate was opened, the sow lifted her wrinkled snout, snuffling and snorting as though fresh air carrying new, enticing scents had found its way into the pens.

"Shoo, now," Maddie said, standing back as the sow sidled toward her through the open gate. Maddie glanced up the road, then down it. The way the road angled, Zeke wouldn't be able to see her unless he walked this way—but she couldn't see him, either. Jake, coming back from moving the milch cows, would be a different matter. She would be able to see him from a long ways off, but he would be able to spot her, too.

Maddie opened the second pen and waited for the sow to come out. The big York hesitated until her companion had ambled out into the road, then they started off together, their heavy bellies swaying. Their soft squeals of excitement made Maddie smile as they headed unerringly for the quarter's garden patches. They would be disappointed to find yet again that nearly everything had been harvested and dried, pickled or salted away—or hidden in the makeshift root cellars Mama had had all the young men digging for the past week.

Maddie watched just long enough to make sure that the sows were headed the right way before she turned and ran back toward the barns, careful to keep close to the line of old oaks again. She slowed before Ginger's barn, staying hidden on the far side of one of the gnarled oak trunks for a long moment before she eased herself around it, still staring at the wide double doors.

"I meet my soul at the bar of God, I heard a mighty lumber . . ."

Zeke's booming voice startled Maddie, and she leaped back behind the massive tree trunk. She pressed herself against the bark, waiting for him to call out a greeting, to ask her what in the world she was up to this morning. But he didn't. Instead, she heard his voice get louder as he came closer. He was entirely absorbed in the song he was singing. When it ended, she could hear his footsteps on the path.

"I had best get started on the grain if Jake has disappeared on me," Maddie heard him say. She exhaled in relief. He was talking to himself. He had no idea she was there. She edged around the tree trunk, her palms flat against the rough bark.

Zeke was carrying a grain bucket, Maddie saw. She held herself very still, poised to draw her head back out of sight if he should turn her way. He went into the barn, and she crossed her fingers. If Ginger tossed her head, or tried to turn and couldn't because her reins held her still, he might notice that she was bridled. Only the dim interior of the barn and his hurry were in her favor.

Minutes after he had gone in, Zeke came back out. He was humming, the big oak bucket swinging lightly. It was empty now. Maddie held her breath, waiting a few more seconds before allowing herself to believe that she was safe, at least so far. He hadn't noticed anything. He'd just gone down the row in a hurry, pouring grain into each manger.

The sound of startled shouts in the direction of the quarter made Maddie tense again. Everything depended on Zeke leaving the stables for at least a few minutes. She eased around the tree trunk until she could see the other direction down the road. At first there were only the muted shouts she had heard at first, then there was a woman's voice, clearly upset.

Maddie saw Zeke stop in his tracks and look toward the quarter. He set the bucket down, then picked it up again and started walking toward the commotion. Maddie could see Albert running up the road, still a long ways away, but shouting in a shrill voice. Zeke started toward him.

The instant Zeke was far enough away, Maddie ran across the road, headed for the barn. She did not slow down until she was in front of Ginger's stall. She flung open the stall gate and nearly fell lunging toward the tied reins. Ginger whinnied quietly, a low, rippling sound that meant she wondered what was going on.

"Time to go," Maddie told her, unwrapping the reins frantically, her hands trembling with urgency. Any second, Jake could come back. When he did, he'd find out she hadn't said a word to Zeke about his leaving with the cows. Maddie could only hope that they would both figure she had decided to go riding and had forgotten.

Maddie knew it was now or never. Using the stall rails, she clambered up onto Ginger's back. It felt improper to sit astride her horse, and she knew her father would never approve. Mama wouldn't, either. It even felt odd and awkward. She was used to the y-shaped tree of her sidesaddle keeping her pegs in place. Still, astride like this, there was a familiarity that was almost unnerving. Until she had been five or so, she had ridden like a boy. She had forgotten how natural and safe it felt.

Holding Ginger on a tight rein, Maddie turned her toward the barn doors. Ginger tossed her head and danced sideways. Maddie sat her easily, feeling the same sense of freedom she had felt when she'd discarded her corset. No skirts, no sidesaddle. Papa would be ashamed of her. But she felt so balanced and secure, even bareback.

At the door, Maddie reined in and then let Ginger ease forward a step at a time. She couldn't see Jake or Zeke, and she couldn't hear either of them, only the muffled shouts down near the quarter. It sounded like the sows were giving everyone a run. They always did. Maddie nudged Ginger forward once more, and they emerged into the sunshine. The road was clear both ways.

Maddie pulled Ginger hard to the left and fought the impulse to urge her into a canter. The sound of hoofbeats would carry, and anyone who heard them would come to look now that they were all so anxious about Yankees.

Scanning the road ahead and glancing behind every few seconds, Maddie kept Ginger in the tree shadows until the road curved to the right around the cotton field. Instead of following it, Maddie headed straight into the woods. Only then, on the soft pine needle-covered ground, did she lean forward and nudge Ginger into a canter. Once again she was taken by the feeling of sheer freedom that the trousers and shirt allowed her.

Keeping Ginger firmly reined in, Maddie wondered at herself. She rode very well sidesaddle. She even followed the hounds sometimes with the neighbor boys, Ginger flying over fallen logs and creeks at a mad gallop—but sitting astride like this was so much easier. She was certain she could ride like this all day and not have the backaches that an all-day excursion in her sidesaddle always left behind. Her mother had quit riding altogether because of her painful backaches. Astride, Maddie realized as she guided Ginger into the pine woods, she didn't have to be wary of being caught in the saddle if Ginger stumbled and fell—a thought never far from any sidesaddle-trapped horsewoman's mind. With one foot tucked beneath the other and the stirrup pinning both, any accident could be disastrously dangerous.

Ginger was frisky and strained at the reins, wanting a good gallop. Maddie held her in, keeping a watch as far ahead as she could, and turning to look behind as often as she dared. It was hard to go very fast in these woods. The pines weren't thick here—these fields had been cleared once, then abandoned when the indigo prices fell sixty years before. The pines had slowly crept back in, her father had told her, but it would be another sixty years before they would be able to take over the land completely again—if her father didn't think of some crop someday that would do well in the wet clay-soil fields.

Maddie felt an odd weight settle into her stomach

as she realized she was assuming that her father would farm this plantation the way his father and grandfather had, and that someday she and her husband and children would take over. It might not be true. She had overheard men saying that there was no telling what would become of the South if the Union army won the war. Lincoln's soldiers were already proving themselves uncivilized. Maybe the land would be confiscated and sold to whomever could bid highest.

Trying to stop thinking about what would come once the war ended, Maddie kept Ginger at a hand-gallop, watching the woods on all sides of them. She stayed alert, her ears straining to catch any unfamiliar sounds. She used the rising sun to keep Ginger headed west. Tossing her head nervously, the mare cantered on, her breathing rhythmic and noisy.

"It's not all that far," Maddie said to reassure herself as much as the mare. "It's walking back that'll be scary," she added aloud, then wished she hadn't.

A distant cracking sound made Maddie twist to her right, startled enough to rein Ginger in, dragging her to a halt. The mare fought the reins at first, then came back into hand. Maddie sat her steadily, listening until the sound came again. Gunfire?

Alert, holding her breath and wishing her heart would quiet itself, Maddie held Ginger still. There. Somewhere west of her was a scattered popping. It was gunfire. Maddie bit at her lower lip. It was a long ways off. If there was fighting, it was still distant . . . and maybe the skirmish would move away from the plantation, not toward it. There was just no way to know, and there was nothing she could do to change anything. The Yankees would come or not, in their own time and from whatever direction they chose.

Maddie urged Ginger back into a canter and kept going as the sounds faded back into silence. For a long while she heard only the thudding of Ginger's muffled hoofbeats. It was a sunny morning, and the trees cast long shadows across the ground. The smell of the pines got stronger as the air warmed.

Maddie wished with all her heart that she was just on the way to Tileys' house or another neighbor's, ready to rehearse some Christmas play or pageant tableau. She had always loved Christmas, until the war had come and changed everything. As she went, Maddie slowly relaxed into the familiar rhythm of Ginger's ground-covering canter. In a quarter hour or so more, she would see the first of the jutting, white rock ledges that would show her the way to her great-grandfather's old house. Then she could get Ginger into the little corral with the creek running through it, give her a hayrick full of the feed Papa kept there, and start home. If she was careful, everything would be all right. No one would see her, and if she saw heard soldiers coming, it would be easy to hide in the trees until they passed.

"You there!"

The shout was so close and so unexpected that Maddie went rigid, her eyes the only part of her capable of quick movement. She searched the trees, turning slowly as she did so, trying hard to spot whoever had shouted.

"Hey! Come back!"

The voice guided her eyes this time, and she saw a corner of something through the trees. It was dark red—not the color of a Yankee uniform at all. Maddie inhaled sharply and reined in without thinking.

"Please!" the cry came again. "I can hear you. You can't just leave me here!"

A cold sweat gathered on Maddie's brow as she pulled hard on the reins. Ginger broke back into a trot, then slowed to a stop.

CHAPTER SIX

Maddie steeled herself and turned Ginger toward the stand of pines. She leaned left and right, trying to see more of the odd patch of red. Blood? It looked like blood. Or just a flannel shirt? She clenched her fists, trying to make out details, but couldn't. Was someone hurt? The pines were too dense to see.

Maddie rode a little closer, then, the pine needles stabbing at her arms through the linen shirt, she slid from Ginger's back and tied her reins to a tree. Her breath light and rapid, Maddie stood very still, looking around once more, searching the pines for any other sign of life.

There were none. Someone had ridden away from this man, had left him on his own. But was he dying or hurt bad and in need of help, or just tired and angry about being left behind?

Maddie started forward, placing her feet carefully so she wouldn't snap pine twigs and give herself away.

"Are you there?"

This time it wasn't a shout; it was as though the man were running out of strength and hope all at once. She didn't recognize his voice, but he could easily be a neighbor, someone she had met at a picnic or a party. Or he could be a Yankee . . . but how could she know unless she got close enough to see if he was wearing a uniform?

"Tell my mother I love her," the voice came again, and Maddie felt her eyes fill with tears. Was he dying, then? He sounded like a Southerner. He had a soft accent that she didn't quite recognize, but she was sure he wasn't a Yankee. A horse whickered from somewhere just beyond the stand of pines, and Ginger would have answered, but Maddie pulled her head around and distracted her, trying to decide what to do next.

If it was a hurt Rebel, some poor boy like Brian Tiley lying wounded, left by the cruel Yankees who had shot him, she wanted to help. It was her *duty* to help. Maddie worked her way closer until the pines stopped Ginger's progress. Then she tethered the mare.

On foot, without the advantage of Ginger's height, she couldn't see the odd patch of dark red she had spotted before. Still, she moved forward steadily and carefully, angling toward the place where the voice had seemed to be coming from. She stopped as she came to a stand of five or six big pines growing so close together that their trunks touched. Trying to steady her breath, she wished the soldier would speak once more, so she could be sure he wasn't a Yankee. The horses nickered again, then one whinnied loudly. They could smell Ginger.

"Oh, please help me?"

Laughter followed, and Maddie spun around to face a man wearing Union blue. His voice was sharp now, and his accent was pure, hateful Yankee. From his right hand dangled a dark red rag, and he swung it back and forth, grinning, then shoved it into his pocket.

"Jeb? Did you find someone to help?" asked a softer voice from the other side of the trees.

"Indeed I did," the Yankee answered, still grinning. "And he's about twelve, maybe thirteen, with hands like a spoiled girl's."

"Well, don't scare him to death, Jeb."

"Anything might. These plantation dandies don't do a lick of work their whole lives," the Yankee said. "They have slaves who do everything for them."

The pine branches shivered as the second man came through them, and Maddie could only stare as he emerged. He was tall and wore a Union soldier's cap. His shirt was stained and worn. If he had a uniform jacket, he wasn't wearing it.

Maddie swallowed. Her throat was so tight that

it hurt. She was all too aware of her hands, with their clipped and buffed nails, and she had to fight an impulse to put them into her pockets. She wanted these men to keep believing she was a boy. If they knew her real gender, they might decide to kidnap her for ransom, or worse.

"You riding bareback, boy?" the first soldier said, walking past her to peer back toward where she had left Ginger.

Maddie nodded, knowing that the timbre of her voice would betray her if she was not careful to speak as low as she could and to say as little as possible.

"Why?" the second Yankee asked. His voice was softer, and his face wasn't filled with hatred.

Before Maddie could answer, the first Yankee spat in the dirt and shook his head. "Why the heck do you care why he's bareback this morning, Andrew?"

The tall man shrugged and grinned. "Because my mind is curious and alert, Jeb. Unlike yours."

"Your mind is idle and flies off on tangents," Jeb said flatly. But he grinned back. It was obvious the two were used to this kind of banter.

Maddie lowered her eyes, trying desperately to think. She had to get back to Ginger. Once she was mounted, she stood a chance of getting away from these men. She often outrode the boys she hunted foxes with. Ginger was fast. She was smart, too, good at keeping her footing in rough country.

Andrew cleared his throat, and she looked up. "Are you riding bareback because you stole the horse but couldn't find a saddle to steal, too?"

Maddie started to shake her head to defend herself, then hesitated, wondering if it was smarter to make them think she didn't come from around here. Her hesitation was long enough to irritate the harsh-voiced Yankee named Jeb. He put his hands on his hips and glared at her. "I asked you a simple question, boy!"

Andrew shook his head and walked away, clearly disgusted. Maddie wrenched around to watch him go. He was headed to where she had tethered Ginger.

"Are you going to answer me?" Jeb demanded. "Or just stand there?"

Maddie glanced at him, listening to the thudding of her own heart. At best, she was going to end up losing Ginger to these awful men, and it was all her fault for being so gullible. How many others had these two men caught by calling out like a hurt soldier in need of help?

"Hey!" Jeb shook a fist at her, startling her. "Answer me when I ask you a question."

Maddie pulled in a deep breath, searching frantically for an answer that would satisfy him without giving away anything about the plantation. "Runaway," she croaked finally, trying to make her voice as low as a boy's. "Stole the horse."

Jeb threw back his head and laughed. "Andrew, he says he's a runaway." He turned his gaze to Maddie's face. "You leave your mama to run off to join the glorious Confederate army?"

She nodded, then shook her head, making him laugh once more.

"Your father fighting?"

Maddie nodded carefully.

To her amazement, the Yankee reached out and patted her shoulder roughly. "You're too young for war. You ought to just go back home."

Maddie heard the sound of hooves and looked up. Andrew was leading Ginger toward her. "We're all too young for war," he agreed. "There ain't a man on earth old enough."

Maddie stood still, staring at Ginger as Andrew stopped. He reached up to pat her neck, and Maddie could tell the gesture was automatic. Andrew always patted horses. Ginger edged forward, extending her muzzle.

"What'll we do with you?" Andrew asked Maddie.

"Can't let him go," Jeb put in. "At least not right away and not anywhere around here."

"Why?" Maddie asked without meaning to. She caught her breath. Her voice had come out too high, but she was pretty sure she had sounded scared, not feminine. Both Yankees laughed.

"Because you are lying," Andrew said quietly. "This horse ain't stolen. She knows you." He let Ginger's reins loosen, and the mare came closer, lowering her head to touch Maddie's shoulder.

Jeb laughed again. "Who'd you steal the mare from, son? Your sister? For all we know, you live just over the next rise and if we let you loose, your neighbors will be out here trying to pick us off before dinnertime."

Maddie felt herself flushing at being accurately called a liar and lowered her head so the Yankees wouldn't see, but it was too late.

"Look at that red face," Jeb said. "I think I just stumbled across the truth. He stole the horse from his mother and left her to fend for herself against us Yankees. Now he's ashamed."

Andrew leaned closer to look into Maddie's eyes. "Is that so? Your mama have a big place around here somewhere with horses and mules and provisions we should know about?"

Maddie shook her head miserably, thinking furiously. "I've been riding three days." She raised her right hand and waved vaguely to the north. Jeb reached out, snake-quick, and trapped her wrist. He turned her hand over forcibly, staring at it.

"You haven't been riding more than a day," he corrected. "Your hands are too clean." He leaned forward to peer into her face. "There ain't a single smudge of dirt or campfire ash on your face, either."

"Washed up in a creek this morning," Maddie said gruffly.

Andrew stared at her, tilting his head. Then, before she could stop him, he reached out and pulled her cap off. Her hair, loosened from riding, slid out of the pins and fell down her back. She snatched Johnny's old cap back and shoved it into the waist of the trousers, then stood glaring at the Yankees.

"We have a bigger problem than we thought," Andrew said quietly. Jeb spat in the dirt and didn't answer.

CHAPTER SEVEN

"Well, now what in blazes do we do?" Andrew said quietly. Maddie glanced up at him. His face was blank with astonishment.

"You let me go," she said, less tongue-tied now that she could use her own voice.

"You, maybe. The mare, no," Jeb interjected, and she spun around to look at him, startling Ginger so that the mare tossed her head and sidled uneasily.

Maddie felt her stomach tighten. "She's mine!"

"I don't doubt that for a second," Jeb said evenly. "But we are assigned the duty of finding horses and mules for General Sherman's army of victorious destruction. We can get you home first, though, if it ain't too far. Where is it?"

Jeb reached out and took Ginger's reins when Maddie didn't answer. Andrew stepped clear, looking up at the sky as though he expected to find an answer there.

Maddie bit at the inside of her cheek. She couldn't tell them the plantation was less than an hour's canter away. If they took her back, they couldn't miss the barns and the horses in the paddocks.

"What's your name?" Andrew said, looking back down at her.

"Maddie Retta Lauren." She said it proudly, holding her head high.

Jeb laughed quietly. "She said that like she was the queen of something or other."

Andrew nodded. "Maybe she is. This is a fine mare. A blooded mare. And that bridle is English leather. Isn't it, Maddie?"

Maddie wanted to take her name back from them, sure that they would somehow find a way to use even that against her now. She glared at them, then glanced at Ginger's reins, held loosely in Jeb's right hand. She gauged the distance, wondering if she could swing up onto Ginger's back the way she had seen boys swing up all her life.

She forced herself to look blankly at the trees, thinking furiously. Neither Yankee was holding one of the coveted repeater rifles everyone had heard about. Jeb had a pistol in his belt. Would he shoot at her if she rode away? She doubted it. They weren't that kind of cold-blooded killers or they would have shot her on sight, when they thought she was a recruit riding to find a Confederate regiment to join.

"Did you let the fire die down?" Andrew asked suddenly.

Jeb shrugged. "Maybe. Why?"

"I wanted to heat water to scrub out my plate."

Jeb made a face. "I can't imagine why you bother. I just lick mine clean and then eat off it again."

Maddie made a small sound of disgust without meaning to.

Andrew smiled at Jeb. "See? You have made the young lady ill with your filthy habits."

Jeb frowned. "I wash my plates at home. What difference can it make here in the war camps?"

Maddie pretended to watch them intently, but she was really only focused on one thing: Jeb's right hand circled the reins so loosely now that it would take only a single tug to free them. But what then? Unless she could mount instantly and wheel Ginger around, they would just grab the bridle and stop her.

"Here," Jeb said suddenly, handing the reins back to Andrew. "Let's do keep that fire going. We may as well roast up that rabbit you shot now instead of waiting for dinnertime. Then we won't have to stop again."

Andrew took the bridle reins, holding them in the same careless manner that Jeb had. He was shaking his head, smiling at Maddie. "You are the last kind of trouble I expected to run into today."

Maddie didn't answer.

"Your pa fighting? Do you have brothers in the war, too?"

He looked at her intently as he waited for her to answer. There was something about the way he tilted his head when he was listening that reminded her of the way Johnny had listened when something really interested him. It was strange to think that Johnny would be almost this man's age now—only a year or two younger. "Papa is. And three cousins. But my brother died swimming four years past," she finally told the Yankee, hoping he would look elsewhere, take his attention off her face. But it didn't work. He only leaned forward.

"Drowned?"

She nodded, refusing to look into his eyes.

"I'm sorry to hear it. But it's better than being shot up like some I've seen," he said quietly, looking aside as though he was talking to himself now, not to her.

Maddie stared at the side of his face. His eyes were shadowed with some awful vision she was glad she couldn't share.

"I saw a man with both legs blown clean off," he said in the same distant tone of voice. "Cannon grapeshot, I suppose." He blinked and shuddered, then focused on her face again and made a gesture of erasure, as though the air was a slate and he could rub out what he had said just seconds before. "Don't mind me, miss. I apologize. And I am sorry to hear you lost your brother."

"Thank you," Maddie murmured.

"Andrew?" Jeb called.

Andrew turned. "What?"

Jeb didn't answer for a second, then did so in a lowered voice. "Riders coming."

Andrew's hand tightened on Ginger's reins. "How close?"

"Close enough to see me if they look—not if they don't. You are both invisible to them, I think," he added.

Andrew gripped Maddie's wrist. "Jeb? Not a word about her. Not one."

Jeb made a sound of distaste. "Aw, Andrew, we should—"

"No. Give me your word on it."

Jeb kicked at a rock. "All right, my word."

Andrew gripped Maddie's wrist and led her into the trees, Ginger following obediently behind him. The pine boughs were prickly, and Maddie turned, trying to find a position where they were not poking through her shirt. "It hurts," she whispered.

"Be still," Andrew hissed at her.

Ginger shook her head, jingling the bridle.

"Keep that mare quiet," Jeb whispered, and Maddie could barely make out his words. "Stand still as stone."

Maddie could hear hoofbeats now.

"Friend or foe?" Andrew breathed.

"Friend," Jeb said faintly, "officers." Then he lifted his voice and called out a hearty good morning. The hoofbeats were broken by a less robust reply. Maddie couldn't make out what the man had said. She glanced at Andrew. He lifted the reins to point at her mouth, covering his own with his other hand. He was warning her to keep quiet. She nodded to show that she understood. He turned to look back through the branches. "Ten or fifteen of them," he murmured. "Three officers. Some kind of official detail."

Maddie tried to follow his gaze, but the difference in their heights meant that she could see only the wall of green pine boughs that hid them from whomever was approaching.

"What are you doing out here, Corporal?" a voice demanded. "Your company somewhere close to?"

"Not far, sir," Jeb said carefully. "My partner and I are scouting places suitable for taking mounts and provisions."

"Have you seen Rebel troops this morning? Cavalry?"

"No, sir," Jeb answered. "Yesterday we did, toward sunset, east of here."

"Wheeler's Cavalry is like a stinging fly," the officer said. "Just big enough to bother. Where's your partner?"

"He's not far, sir," Jeb said. "He was going to shoot us another rabbit for breakfast."

Maddie sank slowly to her knees and peered through the thinner branches near the ground. She could see the stern-voiced man now. He had graying hair and a fierce, angular face. He had on a blue jacket, with fancy braid sewn on it. She could tell by the way he stood that he thought himself important. She couldn't see Jeb's face, but his posture was rigid. Just beyond them, other Yankees sat astride their horses, waiting.

Maddie felt an iron-strong hand on her shoulder and looked up. Andrew gestured emphatically and she stood up, careful not to set any of the branches swaying as she argued silently with herself. Should she cry out for help? Or maybe it was better not to let this Yankee know she was being held prisoner. If he took her from Andrew and Jeb, she would have even less chance of escape.

Maddie leaned back a little and felt the pine needles jab through the linen of her brother's shirt. She pulled in a quick breath but stayed silent, drawing a glance from Andrew. He held her shoulder in a pincer grip, looking down at her fiercely. Maddie nodded, trying to convey to him that it had been a mistake, that she would remain silent for her own reasons, if not for his—whatever they were.

Ginger was standing steadily, but her ears were

flicking back and forth as she tried to take in the sounds and scents of the strange men and their mounts. She blew a soft breath from her nostrils. With a warning look, Andrew released Maddie in order to get a better hold on Ginger's reins.

"When do you report back?" the stern-voiced officer asked.

"Two more days with or without finding horses," Jeb answered without hesitating, and Maddie wondered if it was true—any of it. Were they out to steal horses for the Union troops? Or were they more renegades hoping to find some small treasure in a planter's home that would set them up for life once it could be sold—diamonds, jewelry of any kind, silver candlesticks. Everyone had heard what sorts of things tended to disappear as the Yankees rode through.

"Whose orders are you acting upon?" the man asked.

Jeb murmured some answer that Maddie couldn't hear.

"I wish you luck, then. An army can't be better than its mounts."

Jeb saluted the man on horseback and stood watching as the officer rode back toward his waiting troops.

"Don't move a muscle," Andrew warned her.

Maddie stared at him, listening to the sound of cantering horses. They were leaving. Whether they had been her only salvation or not, she would never know. By not crying out, she had placed her faith in the idea that they promised more danger than comfort. But it was impossible to tell.

"That was close," Jed said quietly after a full minute had passed and the hoofbeats were fading into silence. "I was afraid he was going to send us packing. We do look like we are ripe for being galvanized, I suppose, just the two of us out here."

"Maybe," Andrew agreed. He stepped back out of the lines, pulling Ginger along with him. Maddie followed, rubbing at her arms where the pine needles had prickled her skin.

Andrew grinned wryly. "Maybe we should try it, Jeb. If we turned ourselves into Rebs, we could sure get through this country with more hospitality coming our way."

"Are you deserters, then?" Maddie blurted out. "Galvanized Yankee" was the name people gave to Union soldiers who decided they would fight for the Confederacy instead of their own army. As she waited for an answer, both men laughed, but not nearly as noisily as before.

"No, no," Andrew assured her. "That was a joke, Miss Maddie. We are under orders of the Union army to find mounts and return to guide our company toward them."

"The Confederates have more deserters than the

Union ever will," Jeb said irritably, staring at her. "Jeff Davis pardons them, tells them they are all amnestied. Makes our boys laugh. If he keeps that up, he'll just end up with more and more of his soldiers taking to the hills."

Maddie glared at him. "Too bad the Confederate army doesn't have you running its affairs," she said in a polite tone, meaning to be sarcastic.

Andrew raised his eyebrows, glancing past her to grin at Jeb. "Now you know, she's right? And if they called, he would serve."

Both of the Yankees laughed like fools over the joke, and Maddie could only look aside as though their hilarity was of no interest to her at all. It didn't matter what they thought, she told herself. They were only uncivilized, ignorant Yankees. Her only purpose now was to get away, to save herself and Ginger.

"Where do you live, Miss Maddie?" Jeb asked abruptly.

Maddie was startled and she hesitated a second too long before she managed to answer him. "To the south, about three days' ride."

"You pointed north before," Jeb said tightly.

"No, I didn't." Maddie shook her head, hoping they wouldn't notice that she was blushing. She really didn't lie very well. "Unless I am turned around and I—"

"And where were you going?" Jeb demanded.

Maddie swallowed hard. She had no ready answer for the question . . . why hadn't she had the foresight to make one up earlier in case she was asked? "I wanted to take my mare somewhere safe," she finally said, unsure whether it was smart or foolish to come so close to the truth. "I wanted to put her where Yankees wouldn't find her. She's important to me."

"That much is true," Andrew declared, rubbing Ginger's ears. "It's plain as day the mare loves her. I expect that love is returned."

"I saw her foaled," Maddie said, trying to see deep enough into his eyes to really judge what kind of man he was, but she couldn't.

"I had a dog when I was a little boy," Andrew said, smiling, but wincing as though talking about the dog made him ache. "I would have gone through fire for that big, lop-eared mutt."

Maddie nodded. "Ginger has always been special to me. Like a friend."

Andrew smiled faintly. "Rufus was that and more. I never had another dog as smart."

"Ginger is, too," Maddie said instantly. "Like she knows what I'm feeling. One night when I was really scared because we heard gunfire close by, I ran out to the barn. She just stood quiet and still and let me lean against her and cry for the longest time."

"I have a mule at home that smart. I named him Harry when he was a month old, and it suits him.

Harry looks like he understands what I say to him sometimes." He grinned, and Maddie couldn't help but smile back at him. "I miss that mule more than I miss my own relatives sometimes," he said, laughing.

"You done, Andrew?" Jeb demanded suddenly.

Andrew look startled. "With what?"

"Jawing. We need to eat and break camp and get started, don't we?"

Andrew nodded, but Maddie could see resentment on his face. "Yeah," he answered finally. "Sure. I'll fetch water from the creek."

Jeb jabbed a finger in the air, indicating Maddie. "Fine. And why don't you try not to let her get you thinking about everything we can't think about right now."

"Like what?" Andrew demanded.

"Home," Jeb said flatly. "Dogs we had when we were kids. How scared she is of the war. That old mule."

"There's no harm in it—" Andrew began, but Jeb cut him off with a quick, angry gesture.

"Yes, there is. While you're thinking about your hound Rufus, you're going to be useless. I don't want as my partner a man who's daydreaming about home."

"Then go back and tell Captain Breaker that. He can reassign me."

Jeb scowled. "I don't mean that. But you have to act like a soldier, Andrew. We have to find out where she lives—you're the one who said her horse was worth something. It's probably a big, wealthy place—exactly what we were told to find." He rounded on Maddie. "Where do you live? On a plantation? His voice was low and angry.

"Jeb, don't," Andrew began, but Jeb cut him off.

"Don't what? Don't do our job?" He grabbed at Maddie's shoulder and wrenched her around to face him. "You're going to show us the homeplace. Understand?"

"I won't," Maddie said, her knees shaking with fear. He looked capable of anything, wild-eyed and furious, but she refused to step back and met his eyes.

"Yes, you will!" Jeb shouted at her.

Maddie stood tall, biting the inside of her cheek to keep herself steady. "I won't."

Jeb raised a fist.

"Jeb!" Andrew's voice was sharp, and he came forward tensely.

"Then what do you want to do with her?" Jeb demanded.

"We'll let her go. You can't ask her to play traitor to her own family, Jeb."

Jeb spat in the dirt, breathing hard.

Andrew was staring at him. "This war General Sherman is waging, this idea of ruining the farms and the crops and stealing like cheap-thief rustlers we would hang at home . . . I hate it."

Jeb blinked, his breath still coming hard. "It's orders, Andrew."

Andrew shook his head. "No, it ain't. We were told to scout out stock and horses, not to threaten girls."

Maddie waited, keeping herself still while they glared at each other, their posture stiff and hostile. She almost wished they would fight. If they did, she might have a chance at escape. But then, instead of fighting, they just looked down at the dirt like they were ashamed of arguing. Then each one went about his work.

Andrew took Ginger's bridle off and used a long thong to fashion a halter, then tied her to a tree. Maddie watched, despairing, as he hung the bridle on the other side of camp. Now she had no chance of an easy escape, and there was no way to know which of them would win the argument over what to do with her. Keeping his head down and his eyes averted, Jeb built up his fire, then gutted the rabbit. Andrew saw to the horses, gathering armloads of stiff-stemmed grass from the clearing to one side of the camp. Then he brought a big tin full of water from a little creek a hundred yards off and set it on the fire rocks to heat. Jeb just leaned aside without looking up when Andrew brushed past him.

Without thinking, Maddie felt an urge to offer her help, but resisted the impulse. Why should she help these men do anything at all? They were the reason her world was upside down. They were the reason there were no parties, no joy in the Christmas season. And they caused everyone's fear and Mama's worries. Men just like them were fighting her family's men.

Maddie's eyes filled with tears. She was so afraid for her father. And her cousins were both far too young for war—even Jeb had said that. She missed new dresses—she missed having friends and her cousins' visits and laughing and sleeping soundly at night and picnics and having enough food. She missed *everything*.

Until the war, her life had been safe and easy, even though she had not known or appreciated it. She just wanted to start the day over, to make each decision differently so that she ended up home again, not here in the piney woods, helpless and scared. But she couldn't. All she could do was watch these two Yankees stalk past each other without speaking as they went about their chores, still angry. She looked longingly at Ginger, then at the bridle hanging from the tree limb on the other side of the clearing. Then she wiped her eyes. No amount of crying ever fixed anything. She had to figure out a way to escape.

CHAPTER EIGHT

Andrew was silent for a long time. Then Maddie heard him mumble something, but she couldn't understand what he had said.

"What?" Jeb demanded.

"I said," Andrew repeated quietly, "that I am sick of you telling me what to do and how to do it. You don't hold superior rank. You aren't more than a year older than I am and you are certainly no smarter."

Jeb spat, then turned away for a few seconds. When he came back, Maddie saw the fury on his face again and was sure that Andrew could see it, too. She glanced at Ginger, then across the camp at her bridle, and waited.

The two men stared at each other tensely, and Maddie held still. She found herself hoping again they would get into a fight and give her a chance to escape.

Maddie waited for Andrew to say more. When he didn't, she glanced at Jeb. He was standing stiffly, his fists clenched at his sides. "I don't know what you are talking about," he said finally, and stalked away from them.

"Don't mind him," Andrew said quietly. "He's brooding about a friend who got killed at Spencer's Branch, that's all."

Maddie nodded to show she had heard him, but didn't answer. His voice had gone soft with worry, and he no longer looked angry. "Jeb and me have lived about a half mile apart our whole lives," he explained to Maddie. "Enlisting was his idea. His pa's a firebrand abolitionist preacher back home. We've been soldiering almost two years now."

Maddie nodded again, wondering if he was the kind of person she thought he was. "If I try to leave, will you stop me?" she asked, startling herself with the question.

He nodded. "Yes. Jeb is right about that much."

She stared at him. "Why? How is one girl trying to save her mare from hard use going to—"

"Wheeler's Cavalry is riding all over this country. If they find you and you tell them about us—"

"But I wouldn't," Maddie said, meaning it. "I'm not a spy. And I don't have that much farther to go, anyway. I . . ." She trailed off when she saw interest light his eyes.

"Where were you headed? A relative's place? Is someone expecting you?"

Maddie held very still, trying desperately to figure

out the best answer to give him. If he thought that someone might come looking for her, would he be less likely to try to hold her against her will? She hated lying—and how could she possibly tell which lies would hurt her and which might help?

"Sit the girl down and give me a hand," Jeb shouted. "Unless you don't want coffee and meat?"

Maddie glanced at Jeb. He had the rabbit gutted, the carcass on a stick to hold it above the fire. As she watched, he set up a forked stick to brace the end of his makeshift roasting spit.

Andrew pointed at a flat rock closer to the fire. "Sit down. I'll put your mare on the picket line with our horses."

He led Ginger away, and Maddie felt her throat tighten as the Yankees' horses nickered greetings to her mare. The bridle was hanging on the same side of the clearing as the picket line, but not close enough.

The tethered animals turned as far as they could toward Ginger, breathing in her scent. Maddie watched her mare swish her tail and flatten her ears to let the Yankee mounts know she was not to be trifled with. Then she extended her muzzle toward them.

"You heard him," Jeb shouted at her, startling her into turning to face him. "Come and sit down!"

Maddie swallowed hard and crossed the little clearing to seat herself on the rock. She lowered herself carefully, keeping her posture as stiff as if she had been wearing a corset and a bale of petticoats or a hooped skirt. The trousers made sitting gracefully wonderfully easy, though, and she felt the sharp sense of strangeness again, with the same tinge of jealousy. No wonder men could do more things than women: Their clothes didn't strangle them. She looked at Jeb, wondering at herself. Her thoughts were frivolous, given her situation. She had to figure out what to do.

"I would appreciate it if you wouldn't stare at me," Jeb said, interrupting her thoughts.

She blinked, then blushed. "I didn't know I was."

"That hardly matters to me. Sitting there thinking how much better your family is than we are, little miss—"

"I wasn't," Maddie interrupted him. Jeb looked at her. "I was thinking that men are free to do what they want because they don't have to wear skirts and hoops and corsets."

Jeb squinted, scrutinizing her. "I have a sister who told me the same thing. She's fifteen now."

Maddie nodded. "I never thought about it much until today, but she's right."

Jeb reached out to turn the rabbit carcass over the flames. Maddie could smell the grease dripping into the flames, and her mouth watered. She hadn't brought food. She hadn't meant to be gone from home for more than a few hours.

"Are you hungry?" Andrew asked, walking back from the horses.

Maddie shook her head. She didn't want to eat Yankee food, didn't want to feel like they had offered her hospitality—or that she had accepted it. She was a prisoner, not a guest.

"I want to leave now," she said, meaning to sound adult and insistent, to speak the way her mother had spoken to the Yankees at their door. But she could hear the fear in her own voice. She sounded like a frightened child.

"I'm sorry we can't just let you go," Andrew said as he came closer. "But I'll figure out a way to get you home safe."

"Since you are such good friends," Jeb interrupted him in a tight voice from his position near the fire, "do you want to give her half of your breakfast?"

"What in blazes is wrong with you?" Andrew exploded.

"We meant to trap a Reb, but we ended up with a little girl instead," Jeb shouted back at him. "We can't let her go, but I don't want to take her with us. And *you*, Andrew, are acting like a fool. We should make her tell us where her place is and ride there now!"

Andrew stared at his friend, and Maddie held her breath for as long as she could stand it. Then she spoke into the silence. "If you let me go, I won't—"

"Hush!" Jeb exploded. "Listen!" He jabbed a finger toward the east.

Andrew half stood, looking in the direction Jeb had pointed. A second after he was on his feet, Maddie heard what Jeb had heard. Somewhere off in that direction, men were shouting. Andrew was tilting his head again, his eyes closed as though that would help him understand the faint words.

"Get the horses," Jeb said, getting to his feet. He wrapped the sizzling rabbit meat in filthy cloth and laid it to one side, then began to put out the fire, using a short-handled shovel to throw soft dirt on the flames. Maddie stood up when Andrew did, but was uncertain which way to move. "Stick close," Jeb growled when he glanced up at her. "You can't outride me. Don't try."

Maddie was incensed once more at his rude and bullying demeanor. No one in her life had ever treated her like this. "I will thank you not to speak to me that way, sir," she said, and this time her voice didn't sound quivery.

"Go get on your horse," Jeb hissed at her, his voice low and threatening. "And keep still."

Maddie glanced at Andrew. He had one horse saddled and was turning to the other as she walked closed. He caught her eye as he lifted the second saddle. "Do as he says. Get your mare bridled up. I'll get you home as soon as I can."

Maddie looked off to the east. It was impossible to see anything through the trees, but faint sounds were audible now. Hoofbeats, voices, the creaking of wagon wheels. It sounded like the whole of Sherman's dread army, marching straight toward them.

Terrified, Maddie ran to bridle Ginger. She led the mare to stand beside a rock and stood on it to mount awkwardly, flinging herself over Ginger's back like a sack of pecans, then fighting to swing her right leg over. Once she was up she tucked the reins beneath one knee and used both hands to swiftly twist and knot her hair, putting on Johnny's cap again.

"Stay between us," Jeb cautioned her, then motioned at Andrew. "You stay close to her and make sure she rides hard enough to keep up."

Andrew nodded and swung up onto his own horse. His shirt was stained with weeks of sleeping on the ground, and Maddie saw him turn to untie his blue jacket, tied in a roll like a ground cloth to the back of his saddle. But at that moment, Jeb clapped his heels into his horse's sides, and Maddie heard a popping sound, then a whizzing whine high overhead. Gunfire? Then it wasn't Yankees coming after all?

"Rebs!" Jeb shouted as if in answer to her thoughts, and Maddie could only hang on as Ginger half reared, then leaped into a gallop to keep up with the other horses.

CHAPTER NINE

Maddie leaned low over Ginger's neck as the mare surged into a gallop behind Jeb's horse. Her heart was pounding faster than Ginger's hoofbeats. It *was* gunfire. She could hear a screaming whine overhead that followed the popping sounds by a second or two.

"They won't follow us too far," Jeb shouted over his shoulder.

"Probably not!" Andrew shouted back.

Maddie heard another shot tear through the air overhead and she leaned lower on Ginger's back, her gaze fixed between Ginger's ears, watching the ground ahead for squirrel holes and fallen logs.

Jeb suddenly veered to the right, whipping his horse with his reins. The animal responded with a fresh burst of speed. Maddie looked back. She couldn't see anyone behind them. But the pines were thicker here though. The trees were easy enough to ride through, but they blocked her vision over even short distances. She couldn't hear the shouts anymore, either, or the gunfire.

A slow minute passed as she was lost in the rhythm of Ginger's flying hooves and the rapid thudding of her own heart. When Jeb veered again, this time to follow along a little creek, Ginger made the turn without guidance, her instincts keeping her close to the fleeing horse ahead of her. Maddie sat as far forward as she could, holding the reins loosely enough so that Ginger couldn't feel the bit at all.

A sudden round of the hard-edged gunshots made Maddie flatten herself against Ginger's back, her whole body rigid with fear. If they were Confederates, and they were assuming she was a Yankee like the men she was with, there was no reason they wouldn't be aiming at her, too, their sights fixed on her back at this very second. She wished that she hadn't put Johnny's cap on, but now she was afraid to straighten up and free one hand to get it off.

Ginger galloped hard with no urging at all. Maddie could hear the whining of rifle balls overhead and on both sides of them. She began to pray as Jeb led them on a curving course through the woods, veering to the right again to keep them in the thickest stands of trees.

A sudden low, anguished sound behind Maddie made her wrench around to look at Andrew. A red stain had appeared on his shirtsleeve, the size of an apple. His head was down, and she could see that he had tangled both hands in his horse's mane. He clung awkwardly to his saddle, his balance suddenly labored and uncertain.

"Jeb!" Maddie screamed the name. Jeb turned around, and she saw a look of shock and pain stiffen his face the instant he saw what she was pointing at. He turned and stood high in his stirrups, looking ahead of them, then glanced back at Andrew once more.

"Can you hang on?" he screamed. "Andrew! Can you stay on?"

Andrew lifted his head. His face was deathly white. Maddie felt a stab of anguish go through her heart. But he nodded and answered, "Go on! Don't stop!"

"You watch him," Jeb ordered Maddie, reining in a little. "If he looks like he can't stay up, you call out to me."

"I will," Maddie promised, shouting so he would hear her over the sound of the horses' hooves.

He glanced ahead again, then looked back at her. "Your word?"

Maddie nodded and lifted her chin to shout, "Yes. I promise!" She swallowed hard, unable to stop looking at the bright red stain that was spreading on Andrew's sleeve.

Jeb faced front again. He reined in, glancing back every few seconds, then took a gentler turn to the left. Maddie pulled Ginger in and angled to one side, motioning at Andrew to ride ahead of her, where she could watch him better. Jeb turned in his stirrups, and she saw him scowl. She waved one hand at him, sorry he was so suspicious of her, but unable to do anything about it. He watched long enough to see what she was doing, then turned his head again.

A scatter of gunfire sounded somewhere behind them, but it was farther away now. Maddie let Andrew pass, then fell in behind him. As she did so, her heart constricted. There was a second red stain on the back of his shirt, darker and bigger.

"Jeb!" she called in a tight voice, but Andrew turned to gesture her to silence, a pleading look on his pain-contorted face. Maddie nodded, and he managed a grateful smile. She followed uneasily as Jeb led the way in a long curve to the south, heading deeper and deeper into the woods. Andrew slewed to one side of his saddle, then back, but he managed to keep his stirrups and hung on. Twice Maddie nearly called out to Jeb again, then didn't because both times Andrew managed to right himself.

In a slow, sun-dappled nightmare, they galloped on, the shouts behind them fading into nothing, the pop of gunfire becoming more distant, then stopping abruptly. Jeb veered again and again. On one swooping turn, Maddie saw a jutting pile of white rock that startled her into realizing where she was. They were headed toward the marsh she had meant to reach herself that morning.

She looked back once more. No one was behind them now, or at least not close enough to see. Andrew was still managing to hang on to this saddle, but it was getting harder, she could tell. The wound in his back was bleeding terribly. His shirt was soaked in dark red now. What he needed was a place to rest, a place to regain enough strength to ride back to the Yankee camps and find a doctor.

Andrew did not deserve to die. Maddie was sure of it. He was just a man trying to stay decent and kind in the middle of this terrible war—like her own father. Maddie made a sudden decision.

"This way!" she shouted at Jeb. When he turned to look at her, she pointed, swinging her arm wide. She gave Ginger her head and leaned forward. Ginger responded instantly with a burst of speed that brought her past Andrew's horse. Maddie reined in beside Jeb. "I know the way!" she yelled at him.

"To what?" He was scowling, glancing back at Andrew every few seconds.

"A place where he can rest!" she screamed at him.

He hesitated, then nodded, and Maddie urged Ginger into the lead. Then she reined in, steadily slowing again, glancing back to make sure Jeb positioned himself behind Andrew now. Keeping Ginger at an easy canter, she veered left to skirt the worst of this end of the marsh. "Follow me!" she shouted over her shoulder.

Jeb didn't answer, but she turned to make sure he was riding close to Andrew as they made a wide turn. Maddie was careful to keep Ginger well in hand, to canter just fast enough to keep Andrew's horse from dropping back into a jolting trot. It was obvious he was having trouble hanging on.

The old roads had long since grown over, and unless someone knew them well, it was hard to see where to turn. Following the wide, grassy path that had long ago been a wagon road, Maddie led the way past the old line of broken-down drying sheds that marked the edge of the abandoned indigo fields. She had less and less trouble holding Ginger in; the mare was wearing down, her breathing hard and quick.

"Hold up here," Maddie called after a few minutes more of cantering, but she couldn't tell if Jeb had heard her or not. His eyes were fixed on Andrew, and he didn't answer. Maddie knew why. Having ridden behind his friend, Jeb had now seen the second wound.

Instead of trying to shout, Maddie slowed Ginger gradually, raising her hand the way the huntsman did to get riders behind him to rein in. She brought Ginger down to a trot, pulled her all the way back into a walk, turning in her saddle to watch Andrew as Jeb reached out to grab his slackened reins, bringing both horses to a walk at the same time.

Andrew was badly slumped in his saddle, both hands still on the cantle. Jeb said something in a low voice and then pulled the reins free, leading Andrew's horse. The animal walked with its head down, following Jeb's mount almost blindly. All three of the horses were sweated out, breath heaving, grateful to slow down after the long gallop.

"You sure you know where you're leading us?" Jeb rasped.

"Yes," Maddie said. "My great-grandfather's old house. It's empty now," she added quickly when she saw him frown.

"Where is it? How far?" Jeb asked sharply.

"Not too far," Maddie answered in a voice as cold and sharp as she could make it, trying to match his ugly tone. When Jeb said no more, Maddie turned to face forward and rode on.

The ground got softer, wetter, and the pines gave way to stands of red-barked willow and the oaks that her great-grandfather had dug up as seedlings and moved to plant beside his roads. She hadn't known him, of course. He had died long before she was born. But her father had told her stories about him her whole life. The plantation had been his originally— working alone, then later with the help of her grandfather and his other sons, he had built it up out of pine woods and creek bottoms, one field at a time.

Maddie rode slowly now. Andrew was barely managing to stay upright. The path that curved around the pond was wide and flat and covered with grass and weeds. A few hoofprints would be hard to notice—unless they were gouged in deeply by galloping horses. It was hard to imagine Wheeler's Cavalry chasing too far after a ragtag pair of Yankees and a boy, anyway.

"This way," Maddie said over her shoulder, turning Ginger onto the well-house path. The well was still good, and the water was the sweetest on the place.

"How much farther?" Jeb asked again.

"Half a mile," Maddie said, and she could hear him exhale in relief. She turned to see him reaching out to steady Andrew.

"Is he all right?" Maddie asked.

Jeb made a sound of disgust. "Don't ask tomfool questions."

Maddie bit at her lip. He was so determined to hate her. She tightened her hands on Ginger's reins. It was the Yankees who were marching through *her* home. Her family's plantation. What right did any Yankee have to be angry with *her*?

"You able to make it a little farther?" she heard Jeb ask Andrew in an overloud voice, like he was talking to a deaf man.

"I think so," Andrew answered, but the weakness and pain in his voice were terrible.

Maddie lifted her voice so Andrew would hear as well as Jeb. "My father and his friends use the old place as a hunting lodge sometimes. There are beds and blankets, a good hearth. I can cook a rabbit stew. The old garden still seeds itself—I might find okra or parsnips. And there are apple trees and pecans . . ."

Jeb met her eyes for an instant, and she trailed off.

"If you're lying, I'll—"

"I'm not," Maddie said, insulted. "Why would I lie?"

"Is your father a slave owner?"

Maddie was caught off-guard. She opened her mouth to speak, then simply nodded. "But our people have decent cabins and they—"

"They are not *your people*," Jeb said in a low, ugly voice. He looked aside, and she turned back to face the path.

Maddie rode on, struggling to understand the feelings his words had awakened in her heart. She knew abolitionists felt the way he did. But her father had certainly not invented the peculiar institution. He was not guilty of practicing any of the terrible cruelties one heard rumors about, either. Maddie pulled in a breath, ready to turn in her saddle and defend her father as a kind and decent man, but a popping sound in the distance made her close her mouth tightly, straining to hear. "Was that gunfire?" she whispered, but somehow Jeb heard her. When she glanced at him, he nodded.

At that instant Andrew slid askew in his saddle, and Jeb leaned to support his weight. He grabbed a fistful of Andrew's bloody shirt and hauled him back into a more or less erect position. "Just ride. The quicker we can get out of sight, the better."

"It's right up here," Maddie told him. "Around this next copse of oaks."

Jeb nodded grimly.

"There," Maddie said as they came around the trees. She pointed, and for an instant there was a look of pure relief on Jeb's face, then he saw her looking at him and he scowled.

CHAPTER TEN

The old house was dark. Maddie rummaged through the kitchen until she found some candles and the lucifer matches her father kept in a tin. She ran to the bedroom closest to the front door. It smelled musty, and she heard a mouse rustle inside the wall, but the bed was made up and she saw blankets when she peered into the closet. She pushed the candle down on a spiked holder and pulled open the shutters and the window sash to let in some fresh air. Then she spun around and ran for the door.

Jeb stood uneasily beside Andrew's horse. His own mount and Ginger were in the corral. The instant he saw her, he looked angry. "What took you so long? It hurts him to sit like this."

Maddie came forward, looking up into Andrew's pale face. His eyes were closed, crinkled around the edges like someone with a sick headache trying to keep out every trace of light.

"I'll get him down, but I want you on his other

side when he tries to walk." Jeb's voice had lost some of its bitter edge.

Maddie nodded and came closer. She stood uncertainly as Jeb tried to get Andrew down from the horse. It was a slow, terrible process. Andrew cried out twice, and Maddie clenched her fists. Finally, with agonizing stops and starts, Andrew managed to swing his right leg over the saddle cantle and slide to the ground.

"Help me hold him," Jeb said between gritted teeth.

Maddie positioned herself beside Andrew, ducking beneath his arm, then straightening to fit herself beneath his shoulder.

With Jeb taking most of Andrew's weight, they started forward. Andrew's eyes were still shut tightly, but he managed to shuffle his feet along the ground. Maddie could feel a quivering tremble in his muscles as though he was past any kind of exhaustion she could even begin to imagine.

"Which way?" Jeb asked as they went in.

"To the right," Maddie answered, jutting out her chin in the direction of the bedroom she had chosen for Andrew to stay in.

One small step at a time, they crossed the sitting room and entered the hall. Andrew sagged against Jeb, and Jeb stumbled into the wall. "Help me," he hissed, and Maddie tried to pull Andrew back into a balanced position. Leaning backward with her whole weight, she felt Andrew trying to stay on his feet, too. He didn't open his eyes, but once he was standing solidly again, he squeezed her shoulder and whispered something she couldn't understand.

"About ten more steps," Maddie told him. "Then you can lie down."

Andrew made a sound deep in his throat. And for a second, his eyes fluttered open. Maddie saw him turn his head, taking in the big feather bed, the old bureau against the wall, and the shuttered window. He sighed, a long, shuddering breath.

"Just over here," Jeb said. "A few steps more, old friend."

Maddie heard a warmth in his voice that she wouldn't have believed he possessed. But when he saw her looking at him, his face darkened and he looked aside. Moving awkwardly, the three of them crossed the room and then pivoted with their arms around each other's shoulders like a painful parody of a dance troupe. Then they all three stepped backward, and Andrew sat down on the edge of the bed.

"I'll find something to use as bandages," Maddie said, and Jeb nodded without looking at her.

Maddie lit a second candle from the first and wished this old house had better lighting. Before the blockades had stopped everything, Papa had had coal gas gaseliers built into most of the big rooms at home.

They were bright and smelled less than smoking tal-
low candles. Bayberry candles were better than anything for their scent, but of course no one had been
able to buy them since the war began.

There were bed linens and blankets in the hall
cupboards, and Maddie set the candle onto a wall
sconce as she went through them. She pulled out a
soft sheet with worn edges and tucked it beneath her
arm. She reached up for the candle, then hesitated
and turned back to the cupboard again to pull out
extra blankets. A wildcat had attacked one of the
mares in the spring pasture the year before, and Jake
had begged for every spare blanket in the house,
wanting to keep her warm after her blood loss. Maybe
Andrew would need extra warmth, too.

Hurrying back, Maddie set her candle in a
holder on the bureau. She set about tearing the old
linen into strips a few inches wide. She worked
quickly—she'd had a lot of practice. She could feel
Jeb's eyes on her and wondered if he could tell how
many hundreds of hours she had spent rolling bandages—doing this exact chore—without ever thinking
too much about who the bandages would be used on.

"Hurry up!" Jeb said sharply.

Maddie looked at him and saw that his face was
almost as pale as Andrew's. She handed him the first
roll of bandages, and he looked confused. "You have to
do it," she told him. "It is hardly proper for me to—"

"Proper is the last thing I am worried about," Jeb snapped. "Can you hold him up?"

Maddie shook her head. He handed her the bandages back. "Then you have to do this. I'll get his shirt off."

Maddie started to argue, but she knew he was right. He couldn't do the bandaging alone. But she knew her father would be furious if he ever found out that she had seen a man—and a Yankee at that—without his shirt on.

Jeb unfastened Andrew's buttons and then carefully lifted his wounded arm slowly. Andrew moaned, and Maddie turned her head aside, looking back at the precise moment that Jeb pulled the shirt away from his back. The wound on Andrew's back was oozing dark-colored blood, soaking his undershirt. Maddie looked aside again.

"Come to this side now and brace him up," Jeb pleaded. Maddie held her breath and traded places with him, Jeb letting go his hold on Andrew only when she was in position to take over. A grim frown on his face, Jeb set about working the remaining sleeve down Andrew's arm. When he finally had it off, he dropped the bloody shirt beside the bed. He pulled a knife out of his pocket and cut Andrew's undershirt off. Maddie was sick to her stomach from the metallic smell of the blood, but she bit her lip and helped as best she could.

The wound in Andrew's arm was smaller than

she had expected, but it was terrible to look at. The ragged edges of the hole still oozed with blood. She knew, though, that it was the wound in his back that was dangerous. The darker blood scared her.

Jeb caught her eye. "Bandage him now."

He lifted Andrew's arms while Maddie wrapped the cloth strip tightly around his chest and back.

"Tight," Jeb said. "To stop the bleeding."

"That's what Jake always says," Maddie murmured, more to herself than to Jeb, but he heard her.

"Who is Jake?"

"A doctor?" Andrew managed to whisper between his teeth.

"Our stable man," Maddie admitted. "He always treats the horses and mules, and often people, too."

Andrew laughed, then coughed, a terrible, brittle sound. "Too bad he isn't here."

Maddie nodded and kept her mind on her work, ignoring her uneasy stomach. The bandages seemed to help slow the bleeding from the wound in Andrew's back. She looked up to see if Jeb had noticed and found him staring at her intently. She ducked her head and went on to bandage Andrew's wounded arm. When she finished, she stood back.

Andrew let out a shuddering sigh and spoke without opening his eyes. "You wouldn't think rifle balls were big enough to hurt like this." His voice was faint.

"I'll get a clean shirt," Maddie said, grateful for an excuse to leave the room with its heavy smell of blood and sweat. She ran up the hall to dig through the old-fashioned clothespress in the room her father used when he hunted up this way. She found a thick flannel shirt and pulled it out and hurried back to the guest room.

Jeb had taken off Andrew's boots, and Maddie could see holes in his dirty stockings. She tried not to stare. How awful it must be to live in camps so long that cleanliness and decent clothing became impossible.

"Hand it here," Jeb said impatiently. Maddie wondered, helping him get the shirt on Andrew, how he would do, caring for his friend. Few men made good nurses, Mama said. They didn't have the patience. Mama certainly did. She had nursed Grannie Lauren for years before her death. Maddie had been little, but she had helped—and she had learned a few things about putting an invalid to bed.

"We need to have him stand up and move a little toward the head of the bed," she told Jeb once the shirt was on and buttoned.

He glanced at her sidelong. "Why?"

"It's best if he is a little above the middle so he can just turn and lie back. Once he is lying down, it'll be harder to move him."

Jeb didn't argue with her further. He just helped her talk Andrew into standing, then helped reposition him three shuffling, sideways steps toward the head of the bed.

"There," Maddie said, easing Andrew around so that his back was toward the bed. His eyes were closed, and he hadn't made a sound while they were moving him. "Andrew?" He opened his eyes and focused on her face. "Just sit on the bed, as far back as you can."

Andrew did as she said, and took his arm from her shoulder after another little squeeze of thanks. His eyes were still open, but he was hunched forward, resting his wounded arm on his knees.

"Now," Maddie said once he was seated, "can you turn and get your legs up on the bed?"

Andrew nodded, but had to try three times before he could do it. He made low sounds of pain as he bent his knees and laid himself down. Once his head finally touched the bolster, he closed his eyes and sighed.

Maddie covered him with a blanket, then straightened up to look at Jeb. "If you will give me that rabbit meat, I can make a soup."

He stared at her, and she very nearly asked him if he thought she was going to sprout horns and hooves. Then she caught herself. She had thought that about Yankees, and she still did. But Andrew was different. Or maybe he wasn't, she thought. Maybe the war was full of men trying to be decent and kind, but obligated to go into battle against their natures.

Andrew reached out and took her hand, startling her a little. "Thank you, Miss Maddie."

She smiled at him as he closed his eyes again. Jeb made a sharp gesture, and she nodded to let him know she had seen it—but she didn't move for a long moment. She stood holding Andrew's hand until his breathing slowed and quieted. Then she gently freed herself and followed Jeb into the hallway.

"This Jake. The stable man. Is he white or Negro?"

"Negro," Maddie said in a whisper.

"Then he might help a Yankee."

Maddie nodded. "Jake would help anyone he could help."

"I've seen men with wounds that look like this one," Jeb said, pointing over his own shoulder so she would understand that he meant the wound in Andrew's back. "It isn't good."

"The blood is darker," Maddie whispered.

Jeb nodded. "And Andrew is no coward. If he says the pain is terrible, it is."

"I know Jake has dug stray shots out of the hunting dogs before," Maddie said. "He's no proper doctor, though."

Jeb was staring at her so intently, it made her step back from him. "Do you know one who would come?"

Maddie could only shake her head. "Doc Henders is off with the army, and I don't know another one close enough."

"Who knows if he would have helped a Yankee, anyway," Jake said.

"He might not," Maddie admitted.

"This Jake will come?"

Maddie smiled faintly. "Any Negro man, woman, or child on that place would help you out any way they could. They love Yankees."

"I only hope we are bringing them real freedom," Jeb said, and she could hear the dedication in his voice. "Some are taking advantage of them."

Maddie raised her eyebrows. "Who?"

Jeb hesitated, then spoke. "Soldiers. The Negroes who trail the army . . . it's too many mouths to feed, too slow when the troops need to move quickly. Some soldiers take advantage, get the women to cook or wash their clothes and promise to pay— then don't. The camps are rough. The Negroes end up hungry and dirty and cold at night."

"I hate this war," Maddie blurted out. She could hear the anguish in her own voice and saw in Jeb's eyes that he heard it and felt it himself.

"Maybe afterward someone will sift through and find good things," Jeb said slowly. "Slavery had to be stopped. And that much will be accomplished."

Maddie sighed. "People say it would have ended

on its own."

"Ask Jake if he wanted to wait for that," Jeb said quietly.

Maddie looked askance to avoid his eyes. She would never ask Jake any such thing. Nor would he expect her to feel she should. Or would he? It was a fair question.

"Will you go get him?" Jeb demanded.

Maddie nodded. "Yes."

"How long will it take?"

Maddie hesitated, embarrassed at how brazenly she had lied when Jeb had asked her before. "An hour's ride each way. Maybe a half hour to find him and figure out how we can come back."

Jeb raised his brows. "We?"

She nodded. "He can't come alone. He doesn't know the way. And if any Confederates spotted him, they might assume he was running away. There have been runaways for the past two years. They—"she hesitated, and Jeb filled in the missing words for her.

"Shoot them."

Maddie nodded but raised one hand to keep him from interrupting. "Only if they won't stop and explain themselves, mostly, tell what errand they are on. Or if they run."

"Well, he could hardly explain *this*." Jeb waved a hand in a gesture that included himself and Andrew and everything that had happened to them.

"Maddie?"

Andrew's hoarse, weak voice surprised her. Had he been able to hear what they'd said?

"I'll go catch up your mare," Jeb said.

Maddie nodded, then went back in beside the bed. "I'm going to get Jake to help you."

Andrew closed his eyes, then opened them again. "Don't go." He pulled in a ragged breath. "Too many soldiers out there." He hitched in another breath, then finished. "Dangerous. Both sides." He smiled up at her weakly.

"Can't trust a Yankee," she said, smiling back.

His eyes crinkled as though he was laughing. "Not usually." He tilted his head and looked at her.

Maddie stared at him. "You look a lot like my brother."

"Then I owe him a debt," Andrew whispered. "For his sister's kindness."

Maddie shook her head. "You were kind to me. You didn't steal Ginger. And you wouldn't have let Jeb steal her, either."

He closed his eyes. "Not if I could have stopped him. This war has made him hard."

"I'm going for help." Maddie waited a long moment before he opened his eyes again.

When he did, he stared into her eyes. "Use my saddle. Use my blue jacket."

Maddie pulled in a quick breath. A Yankee

jacket? Mama had thrown away a steel-blue dress because she couldn't bear to have the color touch her skin. "If I see Yankees, can I ask for help?" she asked.

Andrew shook his head and grimaced at the pain the motion caused him. "No doctors up front, even if you could find the army. They're back in the rear now. I can't . . . ride." He paused and took two deep breaths, then looked at her once more without speaking.

"But," Maddie whispered, "what if I see Rebels instead?"

Andrew thought for a minute, then managed a crooked smile. "No jacket. And let your hair down. Tell them you found the Yankee horse in the woods."

Maddie watched his face contort with pain as he closed his eyes. For an instant, she pictured the ugly metal balls lodged in his flesh. The very idea made her wince.

Jeb cleared his throat from the doorway, and she turned to look at him. "You should go now."

Maddie stepped back. "All right."

"Be careful," Andrew said without opening his eyes.

Maddie lifted her chin. "I will. And I'll be back as quickly as I can, Andrew."

He opened his eyes. "I'll repay you somehow, someday."

"You would have helped me, I know it," she responded.

"But I will," he said slowly, "repay your kindness." Maddie waited for him to say something more. When he only closed his eyes again, Jeb jerked his thumb toward the door. On the way out, she told him what Andrew had said about using his saddle.

"I'll have to help you get it on your mare, won't I?" His voice was cold and disapproving, and it made her furious. She was willing to risk her life and put her friend Jake in danger, and Jeb resented helping her saddle Ginger?

Maddie looked at him sidelong. "I have been able to saddle a horse since I was seven years old," she said evenly. "I am sure I won't need to bother you for help, though I thank you very kindly, sir." As she went past him she heard him curse under his breath.

"Which way is your place?" he asked abruptly.

She turned. "Why?"

"If he doesn't make it, I'll ride that way to tell you."

She pointed. "That way, about an hour at an easy canter. But I'll be back soon enough, with Jake. He'll know what to do and . . . " Maddie trailed off, staring at his bleak, impassive face. Was he tricking her now, still intent on stealing their horses? She set her shoulders and walked away from him.

As she crossed the wide, unkempt yard, wading the creeper vines to get to the corral, it occurred to her that her great-grandfather had never owned a slave. Her grandfather had been the first in her family to become wealthy enough to invest in slave labor—and he had had those slaves plant sugar. He had made a fortune in the years before plantations and sugarhouses were common. He would have hated a Yankee in his house. And Papa? Papa wasn't likely to understand. He was fighting the Yankees, risking his life to stop them.

Maddie gritted her teeth and clenched her fists. None of them mattered today. Slavery was wrong. She had written the truth of her heart in her journal the night before. She also knew in her heart that this particular Yankee was a good man. If she could help him, she would. She was at least going to try.

CHAPTER ELEVEN

Maddie felt clumsier in this Yankee saddle than she had bareback. The stirrups were too long, even though she had reset the lacing, and she felt off balance and disconnected from Ginger's familiar gait rhythms.

As she rode, Maddie reached behind herself to touch the heavy blue fabric of Andrew's Yankee jacket again. It fascinated her in a strange way—she had touched it a dozen times already. How many jackets were there like it? How many were worn by men who had shot at her father, her cousins, at young men she had known all her life? Maddie shivered at her own sad thoughts. She longed to take the saddle off, to leave it somewhere and get it when she came back, but that felt wrong, too. Andrew had wanted her to take it.

Coming back through the marsh, Maddie followed the old road part of the way, then took another path she knew about—the old trace into the cane mill

Great-grandpa had meant to build. She didn't want to add to the trail of hoofprints leading to the old place in case Wheeler's Rebel Cavalry came this way, still looking for them.

Maddie sighed as she passed the foundations her great-grandfather had started and never finished. The carefully laid stones ran parallel to the deep creek that flowed at the bottom of the slope. But they were mostly buried beneath creepers now.

Coming back out around the stone outcroppings that marked the entrance road, Maddie reined Ginger in and listened, praying she wouldn't hear voices or the sound of guns. She exhaled slowly, realizing that she was safe, at least for now. There was only silence.

Ginger stamped a forehoof, eager to start home.

"I'm afraid," Maddie said aloud. Ginger shook the reins and stamped again. "All right," Maddie said, letting the mare move forward out of the shadows of the oaks into the sunlight. Ginger flexed her neck, dragging a little slack into the reins. Only then did Maddie realize how tightly she had been holding them.

Turning toward home, Maddie held Ginger down to a ground-covering jog. She didn't want anyone at a distance to see her galloping—nothing would draw attention more quickly. And she left her hair knotted beneath Johnny's cap. It was less odd for anyone to see a boy riding alone than a girl.

Passing beneath the last of her great-grandfather's oak trees, Maddie felt the sunlight thin and dapple, then warm her cheeks again. Her thoughts ran in tight circles as she rode. It was possible that Mama hadn't even really noticed that she was gone. Sarajane had told Mama not to expect her back in the house for a while, after all. The quiet of the woods lulled Maddie into thinking that getting Jake back out to the old place would be easy. She hoped it would at least be quick.

An image of Andrew's white, pain-filled face came into her mind, and she pushed it away. He was warm and safe now. He would be able to rest. Jeb would make him broth and bring him water. If she could just get Jake out there before too many hours passed, Andrew would be all right. Maybe—someday after the war was over—Andrew could meet her parents and tell them what she had done. They would be proud of her once they met him, she was sure. She wondered if her mother would see how much he looked like Johnny.

Maddie was close to home when the sound of hoofbeats startled her. She snapped out of her daydreams and sat straight in the saddle, trying to pinpoint the direction from which the sound was coming. When she was sure, she wrenched the reins to one side and sent Ginger into a gallop, heading for a thick stand of pine trees. Once she was behind them, she dragged on the reins, hauling Ginger to a stop. The mare danced and strained against the pressure of the bit, but Maddie held her still, swinging down out of the saddle.

"Just be quiet, Ginger," she pleaded, leading the mare between two tree trunks that stood about a dozen feet apart. Ginger fidgeted and shied, and Maddie pulled her forward again, trying to seem calm to ease the mare's fears. The mare tossed her head and sidled sideways as Maddie struggled to control her.

"Yankees or Rebels," she said quietly to Ginger, "we want to avoid them all today."

The sound of hooves was coming closer, but there were no shouts, and not a single sound of gunfire. Maddie pulled Ginger farther into the clump of trees, wishing there was a plum thicket to hide inside. Someone looking closely enough might be able to spot Ginger's legs among the trunks—and her own.

Clamping one hand across Ginger's muzzle to keep her from whinnying as the riders passed, Maddie stood close to the mare, hoping to lessen her chances of being spotted. She could see out of the trees if she positioned herself perfectly and peered through the thinnest places in the branches. She leaned one way, then another, until she spotted the riders coming toward her. They were Yankees.

Holding the mare's muzzle tightly, Maddie tugged at the reins to distract Ginger from whinnying. She counted twenty riders as they swept past her stand of trees. They were riding hard, whipping at their horses with quirts or just the ends of the reins. Several of them came close enough for her to see their faces, but their grim, set expressions told her nothing. Whether they were riding away from something or toward something at that breakneck speed, she could not tell.

When the riders were out of sight and the sound of their hoofbeats had faded back into silence, Maddie released her hold on Ginger's muzzle. The mare shook her head, then let the motion go through her whole body, shaking like a dog does to wring water from its coat.

"I'm sorry," Maddie told her. "But if you had whinnied to their horses, the Yankees would have noticed us. And they would take you away from me."

Ginger stood still while Maddie remounted. She cautiously guided the mare out of the pines, her eyes moving over the landscape, scanning the horizon in all directions. Every sound made her start, then slowly relax as she identified it as squirrel chatter or wind high in the pines.

Forcing herself to hold Ginger to an easy pace, and stopping twice more when she heard riders in the distance, Maddie kept going. The ride seemed to take forever. Finally reaching the upper edge of the cotton fields, Maddie pulled Ginger to a halt just in back of the tree line. She waited there, watching the line of horse barns, looking down the road as far as she could see. Then she urged Ginger forward at a quick canter, keeping to the side of the road where the dirt was softer and her hoofbeats not as loud. Once close to the barns, she pulled up again and listened hard for Jake's voice—or Zeke's—but she couldn't hear either one.

"Where are they?" she asked the sky, feeling tears sting at the back of her eyes. The two men were nearly always out in the stables. Maddie wondered about the two sows she had sent waddling down the road. Surely they weren't still out and causing trouble? She shook her head. It had never taken this long for the pigs to be driven back to their pens. Besides, the place was quiet—too quiet, she realized as she rode on at a careful walk.

"Sssst!"

Maddie twisted around in the saddle. At first she couldn't see anyone. Then Sarajane stepped out of the shadowy barn doors. She looked astonished, then puzzled. "I thought you were a Yankee, Miss Maddie. What are you doing dressed like that, riding like a boy?"

Maddie hesitated. "I'll tell you everything, but first I have to find Jake."

Sarajane shook her head. "The cavalry men had everyone out in front of the porch, last time I looked."

Maddie blinked, then slid down off Ginger's

back and led her into the shadowy interior of the barn. "Confederates? Are they still here?"

Sarajane nodded. "I think so. I thought you were some poor Yankee boy about to ride straight into them."

Maddie touched the cap that covered her hair and realized that even without the jacket, up close, anyone would assume what Sarajane had—because of Andrew's military saddle. Her skin prickled. What if she *had* just ridden on down the road and some of the Confederates had seen her? They might very well have shot at her without asking questions.

"I didn't mean I would help a Yankee, really," Sarajane was saying.

Maddie smiled at her. "Oh, yes, you would, you'd be a fool not to."

Sarajane's eyes opened wide. She hesitated a long moment, then shook her head. "All this is so hard, Miss Maddie," she said carefully.

"It's terrible," Maddie agreed. Then she began to tell Sarajane what had happened to her that day—and what she meant to do now. Before she was finished, Sarajane was interrupting her.

"That's why you want Jake? To help doctor up that Yankee?"

Maddie nodded. "Has Mama missed me? Did you tell her I'd be out here?"

Sarajane nodded. "I told her. Whether or not

she's had even a minute to think about you, I don't know. The Confederates came thundering down the road about an hour ago."

Maddie brightened. "That long ago? Maybe they're gone."

Sarajane shrugged. "Daisy came running out back to tell me to close up the springhouse and get away from it. They wanted food. I closed it, then I came back here and hid. I am just so scared of all of them."

Maddie put her arms around Sarajane and fought to keep from crying. She could feel Sarajane trembling. "What if I get scared when the Yankees come, too," Sarajane murmured. "It won't matter, will it?"

Maddie was puzzled. "Matter?"

"If I get scared and hide when the Yankees come, it won't mean I am not set free, will it?"

Maddie shook her head emphatically, furious with herself for not realizing the quandary Sarajane was in. "Oh, no," she said quickly. "If they win, they say they will free all the slaves. And everyone is saying they'll win soon."

Sarajane looked weak with relief. "Your mama told my father we can stay or go as we please after it's all over, but it is so important, and I . . . "

She trailed off, and Maddie tried to imagine what she must be feeling. This war seemed to torture everyone. Maybe every war did. Maddie tried to think of something to say, but Sarajane hugged her again, and that seemed better than any words could ever be.

When they stepped apart, Sarajane took a deep breath. "I'll go find Jake."

Maddie looked into her eyes. "I thought you were scared to go out there."

Sarajane nodded. "I am. But this Andrew Yankee didn't let being scared stop him from fighting, did he?"

Maddie felt her eyes stinging, and she cleared her throat. "No. He didn't." *And neither did my father, nor any of the other soldiers fighting, because they believe in something,* she said within herself. Then she said a silent prayer for her father's safety and her cousins, and all the other soldiers on both sides.

"Dressed like that, your mama wouldn't know you, if you stayed far enough away," Sarajane said slowly.

"Then I will," Maddie said. "I won't get closer than I have to, but I'll go with you."

CHAPTER TWELVE

They came around the corner of the house and saw the last of the Rebels headed down the road. Staying behind the honeysuckle vines that mounded up and over the porch trellis, Maddie watched her mother. Mama stood with her hands on her waist, just above the belled outward curve of her hoops. Even at a distance, Maddie could see she was pink-faced and upset.

"There's Jake," Sarajane whispered. She pointed, and Maddie followed her gesture. Jake was standing with Auntie Mary and Albert and Zeke. Some of the others were walking away. Everyone had their heads down and moved slowly. Maddie understood why—in a way that she wondered if she would have the day before. They didn't like seeing Mama upset and bullied and they hated giving up any of the food they'd worked so hard to store. But more than any of that— the presence of the Confederate Cavalry made freedom seem less likely.

"You stay here," Sarajane said softly. "I'll go fetch Jake."

Maddie nodded her thanks, and Sarajane stepped out from behind the vines, running a few strides, then falling back into a natural-seeming walk. Maddie watched her mother turn back toward the house. When she spotted Sarajane, she cupped her hands around her mouth. "Did you see Maddie back there?"

"Yes'm," Sarajane answered.

Mama frowned. "What is she doing all this time?"

"She was with that mare of hers, mistress," Sarajane answered. Maddie wondered how often Sarajane had had to lie like this in her life. Hiding something she didn't want to get in trouble for by telling just part of the truth.

"Jake!" Mama called.

He turned. "Yes'm?"

"When you see that daughter of mine, tell her no more than another hour or two with that fool horse. I need her help in the house." He nodded, then said something to Zeke, who started back toward the quarter, walking the fencerow on that side of the yard.

Maddie watched as Sarajane called to Jake. He stopped and waited for her. Then Maddie noticed that her mother had turned and was walking back toward the house. Maddie crouched down until she heard the front door swing open, then shut again. Once she knew Mama was inside, she stood up again, peering through the tangle of vines. Jake and Sarajane came toward her slowly, then appeared around the sprawling honeysuckle.

Sarajane was just winding up the explanation. Maddie added to it, talking in a low voice as they all three walked cautiously back around the house and headed toward the barns.

"I'll go," Jake said simply when Maddie finished.

Maddie hugged him, and he half picked her up, then set her down quickly. "Sarajane, tell Zeke the truth about all this, no one else. In case we run into them cavalry boys, I want someone to know what became of me." Sarajane kissed Maddie's cheek, then ran toward the quarter.

Out at the barns, Jake saddled a tall gelding, whistling softly the whole time. Maddie could tell he was nervous. He tied his old saddlebag across the back of the saddle. Maddie knew it held his doctoring tools—needles and thread, a sharp, slim knife, bandage rags, and more.

"Andrew is a good man," she said aloud. "You'll see. And his friend Jeb is all right, too. He's an abolitionist."

Jake swung up on the gelding without saying anything, and they started off. Only once they were past the tree line and out of sight from any at the plantation did he face her. "I've never seen an abolitionist. Preacher Hall says they are evil when he visits the praise house. Your father said he'd run them off if any came around."

Maddie swallowed hard. She hadn't known that. How many other things hadn't she known?

"All the planters run off abolitionists," Jake added when she didn't answer. "Not just him."

Maddie tried to think of something to say, but couldn't. "I'm sorry," she said finally.

Jake turned to her with an expression of puzzlement. "For what? You're a child."

Maddie had no answer for anything he had said. She had no answer for her own spinning thoughts. She kept Ginger at a steady canter, less afraid of attracting attention now. A boy and a slave out in the woods looked like they were running a neighbor-errand, an everyday occurrence in this country. From a distance, no one would notice her Yankee saddle or the rolled-up jacket she was taking back to Andrew. No one would be likely to stop them and ask their business.

"Tell me about his wounds," Jake said as they rode.

Maddie described the ugly, ragged hole in Andrew's arm, then the one in his back. "And the blood from that one was dark." She saw Jake stiffen, then he looked at her. "That don't sound good, Miss Maddie."

She started to say something more, but he touched his heels to the gelding's sides, and she had to urge Ginger into keeping up with the fresh horse so she could lead the way. She kept scanning the horizon, and once thought she saw a rider, but Jake galloped straight on, without so much as looking left or right. She called directions out where they needed to veer or turn to follow one of the creeks.

When they got close, Maddie pointed at the outcropping that marked the old road. "See the white rocks?"

Jake nodded. "Is that one of your Yankees?"

Maddie stared into the shade beneath the oaks beside the old road and made out the form of a rider. It was Jeb. Feeling her heart constrict, Maddie reined in and Jake followed her lead. As they slowed, Jeb emerged from the shadows of the oaks.

Maddie bit her lip as Ginger fidgeted. "Jeb, this is Jake," she said, making introductory gestures.

Jake lowered his head. Maddie knew he was as nervous meeting a Yankee as she had been. "Nice to meet you, mister . . . "

"Jeb will do, Jake. I thank you for coming."

"I hope I can help," Jake began.

"You can't," Jeb said sharply, and Maddie's heart skipped a beat. Jeb met her eyes, and his voice softened. "Andrew is gone."

Jake let out a long breath, and Maddie could

only stare, unable to believe it. "He died?"

Jeb nodded, and Maddie's eyes ached with tears. She had known he might die, but she hadn't allowed herself to think it might really happen.

Jeb looked up at the sky, then back at Jake. "So long as you came, I'd as soon bury him here as take him back."

It was only then that Maddie noticed Andrew's horse, still tied to the oak tree. Across its back was a man-sized bundle. Jeb had wrapped Andrew's body in a quilt from the house, tied with a netting of twine from the shed.

Fighting her tears and the weight inside her heart, Maddie followed the two men back to the old house. She stood off to one side while they found spades and picked a spot below the corral to bury Andrew. Maddie watched as they worked side by side, digging in a steady rhythm until the grave was deep and straight.

"If you know a hymn, he would've liked that," Jeb said, looking at Maddie after they had lowered Andrew's body into the ground. "I can't sing or quote the Bible just now. My father would be ashamed of me, but I can't. Andrew was my friend since . . . " He trailed off, and Maddie could see he was fighting his emotions.

"I would be honored to sing," Jake said in a careful, polite voice.

Jeb nodded, and Jake began one of his beautiful praise-house songs. Maddie joined him and lifted her voice as well as she could. It hurt to sing. It hurt to be alive, to be standing by the grave of someone she had cared about. She glanced at Jeb, who stood with his hat off and his arms crossed over his chest, stiff and silent, his eyes closed. Andrew had said Jeb had been grieving one friend. Now he had lost two.

When the hymn was finished, Jeb said a prayer. Then the men began to fill in the grave. After a time, Jake handed Maddie the spade, and they let her put a few spadefuls in. She found herself shaking so hard that Jake gently took the spade back from her. He and Jeb worked while she stood, numb, staring without really seeing anything.

Jake left the last of the burying to Jeb and went off toward the house. Maddie blinked back tears as he passed her. She clenched her fists, suddenly angry. She wished she had never run into Jeb and Andrew. Maybe they could have ridden faster without her. Maybe if she hadn't been with them, they would have turned and fought. Maybe—

"Stop it," Jeb said quietly.

Maddie looked up, startled out of her thoughts. "What?"

"Stop blaming yourself. A soldier learns that. You can't tell why some die and some don't. No one can."

Something in his words freed Maddie's heart,

and she began to cry hard. Jeb came to stand awkwardly beside her, reaching out to take her hand as she sobbed. When Jake returned, carrying a white stone so heavy, he could barely walk with it, Jeb stepped back, releasing her hand. Maddie mumbled a thanks, and he nodded.

Jake set the stone at the head of the grave, then turned to hold Maddie close. He didn't say a word, but he swayed back and the motion comforted her. After a long time, she dried her eyes and straightened up, sniffling and managing to look up at Jake. He patted her cheek. "You were brave. You did all you could."

"No one ever gets to say more than that," Jeb said, and the sharpness had come back into his voice. He looked at the sky. "Time for me to start back."

Maddie nodded. "I'll put Andrew's saddle on his horse."

"Leave it," Jeb said. "He told me to give it to you when you came back."

Maddie took a shuddering breath. "He did?"

"He didn't have anything else." Jeb walked to his horse and swung up.

Maddie managed to get on Ginger and ride after him. Jake brought up the rear. Twice, Maddie saw Jeb glance back toward the grave, then he just rode onward. At the outcropping, he touched his hat in a gesture of farewell, then galloped away.

CHAPTER THIRTEEN

They were nearly home when they heard the hoof-beats. Maddie wrenched around to look behind them. The sound was incredible, swelling into a thunderous noise. Jake reined in, then leaned forward and reached out to slap Ginger's rump. "Ride!"

Awkward in the too-long stirrups, Maddie fought to stay on as Ginger leaped into a gallop. Jake rode behind her, switching at his gelding with the ends of the reins. Maddie knew he was not afraid of meeting Yankees—or, at least, not very afraid. It was the idea of Confederate troops suspecting him of running away or helping the Yankees that scared him. She leaned forward and forced her tired mare to gallop a little faster.

The hoofbeats behind them dimmed as the seconds ticked past. Maddie swerved around a stand of trees and looked back. She couldn't see riders. Maybe no one had seen them. As they rode from the woods and pounded down the road toward the barns, Maddie looked back again. No one was following them. They had made it home safe. Reining in by the barns, Jake swung down and glanced up at her. "I'm going to get this horse put away quick before anyone sees." He paused and looked at the tree line. "If they weren't coming fast, with that noise—"

"Then there must be hundreds of them," Maddie finished for him as he flipped up the stirrup to loosen the cinch. "But I think they've just gone past us," she added, staring at the trees a half mile away.

"I hope so," Jake said.

Maddie nodded. Ginger stood with her head down, blowing long breaths that riffled the dust. "She's tired."

Jake didn't answer for a few seconds, looking up at the tree line, then back at her. "I'll come back and walk her cool, Miss Maddie. Or she'll be stiff tomorrow."

"I can do it." Maddie tugged Johnny's cap down tighter over her hair. In a few minutes she would have to turn herself back into a proper girl and go back to the house. She imagined walking in and acting like nothing had happened, and felt her eyes sting. She was in no hurry to face her mother.

Jake raised his eyebrows. "You all right?"

She shook her head. "But I will be, I think."

He considered her for a long moment. "You are

braver than most, Miss Maddie." He looked past her. "Like your mama." He patted Ginger's neck. "I'll go see to the brood mares, then."

As Jake left, turning the gelding out into the second paddock, Maddie began to walk Ginger in a wide circle, starting to cry again. She couldn't make sense of anything. Everything was askew, broken beyond repair.

The sound of a trumpet call jerked Maddie around. She stumbled to a halt and could only stare as a line of blue-coated soldiers materialized from the pines. Behind them was another line, and behind them, another. Maddie stood frozen as they came forward in rank and order, jogging their mounts across the cotton fields, some of them pointing at the horses in the paddocks.

An officer shouted an order, and the sea of approaching Yankees divided itself into two groups. One rode past the paddocks on the far side, going into the orchard and on toward the house. The other slowed their mounts just above the barns and began dismounting, rallying around a single man. "Empty the paddocks," he was shouting. "Leave anything old or feeble. Leave any mares close to foaling."

Maddie pulled Ginger around in a tight circle and started for the barns as he went on shouting at the soldiers. Maybe if she could hide Ginger inside somewhere. Maybe . . .

"Keep yourselves orderly. No shooting unless someone shoots first."

The knot of men broke up and fanned out. Desperately, Maddie dragged on the reins, trying to make Ginger trot, but the mare was too tired and too distracted. She balked, turning back to look at the mass of blue-coated soldiers. The commotion rose to an uproar in seconds as horses were driven out of their paddocks. Maddie jerked at the bridle.

"Don't abuse that mare, boy."

The voice came a split second before a heavy hand closed on Maddie's forearm. She looked up into a soldier's face. He looked exhausted.

"Are you supposed to be walking that mare cool?" he demanded, turning to run one hand over Ginger's sweat-soaked coat. Maddie nodded without speaking, afraid to say anything aloud.

"Then take her up there, away from the noise," he said reasonably, pointing. "We'll be off before long, and the soldier is going to need his mount."

Maddie nodded again and swallowed hard as he walked away. She led Ginger toward the foaling barn, weaving her way through the soldiers who streamed across the road like summer ants. They glanced at her, some of them, but none gave her more attention than that. They all seemed to assume what the first Yankee had: She was a stable boy who had been ordered by a Yankee to walk a sweaty mare.

It was incredible how quickly the barns and paddocks were emptying. Maddie saw Jake talking to one of the Yankees at the door of the foaling barn as she circled Ginger, keeping her head down. The Yankee turned and walked away, and Maddie saw Jake stare at her, then purposely look aside.

Maddie turned her circle again and when she faced the barn, Jake was still there, busying himself with unneeded raking, where he could keep an eye on her. Exchanging glances every time she came back around, they could only wait until the last of the Yankees had ridden out of the barnyard.

Maddie led Ginger toward Jake, her knees trembling. He hugged her for a long moment, then stepped back. "Some of them are probably still up at the house bothering your mama. Let's get the mare in here."

Maddie led Ginger inside, and they unsaddled her quickly, turning her into one of the big foaling stalls. Then Maddie ran to get her clothes from behind the hayrick in the third barn. Once she was dressed, she stepped back out into the last of the afternoon's sunshine. It was cooling off fast, and she shivered. Jake put his arm around her shoulders as they started for the house.

"Andrew's saddle was what saved her," she said quietly.

Jake squeezed her shoulder. "I suspect he thought about that."

Maddie started to cry again, and he slowed, giving her a moment to dry her eyes. "Your mama doesn't need more worries."

Maddie nodded. He was right. She straightened up and took a deep breath. Her hoops and skirts felt unfamiliar now, and her corset pinched at her waist. Jake walked her to the back door and opened it, then stood back as she went inside.

"There you are!" Daisy exploded the instant Maddie walked into the kitchen. "The Yankees are out front asking your mama where the stores are hidden. She won't tell them."

Maddie went to the door and looked out. Her mother was standing toe-to-toe with the officer again, just as she had that morning. This time, Maddie didn't hesitate. She swung open the door and went to stand beside her mother. Mama seemed startled, then she laid one hand on Maddie's shoulder. "We need that food," she was saying.

Maddie cleared her throat. "My mother is thinking about the babies and the old people, sir. Most of them will stay with us through this winter, and we all have to have something to eat."

Mama looked down at her and smiled, then she

looked at the Yankee, her head high and her shoulders squared. "That is what I have been telling this officer, Maddie."

The Yankee swore softly, then pivoted and walked back to mount his horse. He shouted an order, and the troops turned back toward the road, driving the horses before them.

December 12, 1864

I could not write last night. I could only cry. This morning I ran out to be sure Ginger is still here. She is. Jake slept in the first stall to watch over the mares. Neither he nor I said a word about Andrew. I will always be grateful to Jake for risking his life to help. I am thankful that at least he was not hurt in all that happened.

The Yankees took all the other horses, but missed the milch cows. They took the sows. Mama managed to keep most of our hidden provisions secret. Today we can see smoke to the southwest. I think they have passed us and will not come back.

I want to record something here, in case my grandchildren should ever read this journal. Andrew, a Yankee soldier, is buried on the old place, at the foot of the oak that stands nearest the creek, straight out from the front door. There is a stone marking the grave. He helped me keep my mare and was a good and honorable man. I will write the whole story perhaps later, when I can stand to. For now, I want to write this much:

I was thinking last night about all the soldiers who have died far from home. Thousands have been buried by friends or strangers, in every battlefield and town and pasture across the whole country. My hope is that those graves are honored, and all the earth in which they lay. And if there is cause for another war someday, please remember this one and all who died, on both sides, and do whatever you must to avoid it.

Sometimes one day can change a life forever

American Diaries

**Different girls,
living in different periods of America's past,
reveal their hearts' secrets in the pages
of their diaries. Each one faces a challenge
that will change her life forever.
Don't miss any of their stories:**